TWISTED FATE

A Dark Mafia Romance

BECCA KANE

BlackRose Books

Book Description
TWISTED FATE

DANGEROUS. VICIOUS. TWISTED.

ALINA

I'll do anything to protect my brother, even willingly become the captive of a man like Damian Russo—criminal, killer, villain, Mafia Prince.

If I try to escape, my brother dies.

I don't want to want Damian, to crave him, to ache for his touch. But that doesn't stop him from summoning my darkest desires.

I'm afraid I'm losing myself completely to him—body and soul.

DAMIAN

Alina Madsen is my prisoner. She believes she's just collateral, a guarantee her brother will pay his debt.

But she's a pawn, a game piece in my quest for vengeance against her ex, the man who killed my father.

I'll use her, take her, enjoy that gorgeous body while I force her secrets from between those luscious lips.

At least, that's the plan, until the primal part of my brain rears its head and roars, ***Mine.***

*****Twisted Fate** is the first book in the **Vegas Vicious** series. It is a stand-alone romance in a connected series featuring the Russo crime family. Enemies to lovers, captive heroine, obsessed alpha billionaire hero. This full-length novel includes violent scenes, profanity, and explicit sex. May not be suitable for sensitive audiences.***

Also by Becca Kane

The Vegas Vicious Series

—Dark Mafia Romance—

Twisted Fate

Ruthless Vow

Dark Promise

Bonus Content

Double or Nothing, a Twisted Fate Bonus Epilogue

Twisted Fate

www.BeccaKane.com

1

Alina

A HAND CATCHES MY ARM—STRONG, commanding, a searing touch. The kind of hand you don't pull away from if you know what's good for you. Long, strong fingers. Neat, trimmed nails. The tattoos on the hand—a fearsome skull on the back, the ace of clubs between the thumb and forefinger, a small cross at the base of the fourth finger—are a stark contrast to the diamond-studded Patek Philippe watch peeking out from beneath the cuff of an expensive black jacket.

"Who are you?" The voice is low, sexy, intimate somehow even here in the crowded casino amidst the hoots and shouts and ringing of slot machines. There's a reason for that ringing. It makes people think that someone just won, and if someone won then *they* can too. So they feed their money into the machine again and again and again, desperate for the win that never comes.

"I'm nobody," I reply, keeping my eyes on the carpet beneath my feet—gold carpet with dark red flowers—willing the guy to walk away. I don't look around for Enzo; I hope he's still doing whatever he's been doing for the past half hour while he left me here waiting. This is not the moment I want him to arrive with his hair-trigger temper.

"Nobody? I find that hard to believe. Tell me your name." The stranger's words are a command. One I have no intention of following.

"Nobody," I say again, but then make the mistake of raising my gaze. His eyes are as black and cold as a demon's, but set into the face of an angel chiseled from marble. Thick, dark hair. A straight slash of brows. Three-day scruff that's artfully maintained. For what feels like a small eternity, I'm trapped, locked in that dark gaze.

Bad boys are my kryptonite, so in different circumstances, I would do exactly as he commands and tell him my name—Alina Madsen—along with my number, my address, and any other pertinent information he might want. I am tempted, so tempted.

But I know exactly what Enzo's reaction will be if he finds me talking to a man, any man, especially one who looks like this. Fists first, questions later.

How did I not realize that sooner?

I met Enzo a couple of months ago, soon after I arrived in Vegas. He was charming, handsome, and had very deep pockets full of wads of cash that he liked to spend on taking me out to nice places. I foolishly hadn't questioned where any of that cash came from. Let's call it a hard lesson learned.

After overhearing snippets of a few business calls, I realized he unofficially worked for the Ivanov family. The Russos and the Ivanovs—two powerful crime families, constantly at war with each other for absolute control over this city. It felt like a world—or, underworld, really—that only existed in the movies—The

Godfather or The Sopranos. Not exactly on my everyday radar.

Funny thing about hard lessons, they often come in pairs. The first time Enzo lost his temper with me because some guy was looking at me and he thought I was looking back, he yelled. Then apologized. And I accepted.

The second time, he punched the wall beside my head. Then apologized. And I accepted.

The third time, he grabbed my shoulders and shook me. He apologized. I didn't accept…until I did. Stupid me.

The fourth time, he bruised my wrist and yanked my arm so hard it left my shoulder aching for days after. He apologized.

I didn't accept.

But he kept calling, swearing he would never lay hands on me again. Finally, I agreed to meet up with him here tonight, a busy casino with lots of witnesses and security where I can tell him in person that we're done. I figure that if he sees my face when I say it, sees that I mean it, then he'll finally get the message and leave me alone.

That's my goal, and the last thing I need is to give Enzo an excuse to lose his shit.

Hoping he hasn't seen me, I look around for him. I don't see him, but I do notice the two guys standing just behind the demon-angel. They're all tall, over six feet. And they're insanely good looking. One has light brown hair and green eyes, his nose straight and a little narrow, his features perfect. A little too perfect for my taste. The other one's blond with blue eyes, his hair thick and wavy, his mouth curved in a smirk. Despite the different coloring, there's something similar about all of them… the cheekbones or the strong jaw… I wonder if they're related.

A buffet of gorgeous.

But it's the demon-angel who holds my attention.

I glance down at his hand on my arm and reluctantly pull away. "I'm meeting someone," I mutter.

The guy's grip isn't tight and I remove it easily. Clearly not taking the hint, he reaches for me again, lean muscle shifting under his impeccably tailored suit jacket.

"Lost your charm, bro?" the blond asks with a laugh and punches him in the shoulder.

I take the opportunity to spin and flee, ducking around a line of slot machines, skirting a waitress carrying a tray laden with drinks, before weaving through a group of girls who look like they're in Vegas for a bachelorette, if the flowing white veil one of them is wearing is any indication.

After a minute, I peer past the machine we're all clustered around and see that the demon-angel is gone. In his place stands Enzo, his face a mask of rage.

He storms over and grabs my wrist in a crushing grip that will leave marks. So much for never laying hands on me again.

Despite my protests, he drags me through the casino and shoves me through a set of doors. And so much for the safety of witnesses and security. The doors swing shut behind us, leaving us alone in a huge, dimly lit banquet hall, empty except for stacks of chairs against the far wall and a single table bearing an empty bottle and two dirty glasses.

I yank my arm free. His fingers have left red imprints on my pale skin.

"Do you know who the hell that was?" he yells, raking his hands through is hair.

"Who?" I snarl at him, rubbing my wrist.

"That was Damian Russo and two of his brothers, you stupid bitch."

I stare at him for a moment, my heart racing. Then I brazen it out. "I'm supposed to know who Damian Russo is?"

Before Vegas, I was just a normal girl who'd grown up in Buffalo, New York. I'd been an A-student in high school and was in the process of earning my degree in English Lit from a local university when Mom and Dad got hit by a drunk driver on the way back from their regular weekly date-night dinner. The coroner said they died instantly.

For some people, the familiarity of home—the house they grew up in, the park around the corner, the stores and buildings and neighbors—might ease their grief. For me, it only made it worse. Besides, I couldn't afford the rent on the house. I developed a whole lot of wanderlust. So I started traveling, and eventually I ended up here, in the middle of the Nevada desert. Partly because I like the heat, the energy, the town that never sleeps, but mostly because it's where my brother Markus ended up and he's all the family I have left.

For a hot minute, it was a loving reunion. Markus hugged me, fed me, let me stay at his place rent free until I got a job and found a place of my own. He joked that I'd keep him out of trouble. He was so happy to see me. So happy to have me around. Until he wasn't, because I started asking too many questions and the answers told me my brother was up to his old tricks. Drinking. Using. Gambling. Hanging out with a very wrong crowd.

Between things both Markus and Enzo have said, I know exactly who Damian Russo and his brothers are: Mafia royalty.

"Russo is the wrong man to flirt with." Enzo glares at me, his face red, a vein throbbing at his temple.

I let out a humorless laugh. "I wasn't flirting."

Without warning, he backhands me, leaving my ears ringing and the taste of blood in my mouth. I stumble back and stare at him with shock. "What the fuck—?"

"He's a coldblooded killer," Enzo snaps. "You cross him, and you die. No exceptions."

"Gee, thanks for the friendly warning," I mutter, my hand pressed to my burning cheek. I cut a glance at the doors and take a step toward them.

"I saw how he was looking at you," Enzo says, pacing now.

I sidle closer to the doors. *How was he looking at me?* I don't ask, not wanting to feed Enzo's rage.

He stalks toward me, blocking my path and answers as if I did ask. "Like he wanted to fuck you." Again, he rakes his fingers through his hair. "Stay the hell away from him."

I guess I'm feeling more anger than common sense right now. "Or what?"

The look Enzo gives me is, in a word, soulless. I know I've said the wrong thing. And I'm pretty sure Enzo's already lost every last one of his morals doing who-knew-what for who-knew-who. For all of Vegas's shiny, glossy exterior, it's only a cover for the bottomless pool of darkness that lies beneath.

Enzo is part of that darkness.

For each step I back away, he stalks a step closer. My mouth is dry. Fear makes my chest so tight I can barely breathe. My pulse pounds. I slip my right hand back and reach… reach…

Enzo lunges for me. I swing the empty bottle I'd grabbed from the table at his temple and I run.

I tear through the doors and plunge into the crowd, not daring to look back. Then I see him, Damian Russo, standing near the bar, staring right at me. For a second, I have the weird thought that if I run to him, he'll protect me from Enzo. And that is probably the craziest thing that's ever crossed my mind.

His dark eyes narrow as he stares at me, anger flickering across his expression. Then the man beside him puts a hand on his shoulder and Damian turns his head.

A glance back reveals Enzo staggering in my wake, fingers pressed to his temple as he searches the crowd. He hasn't spotted me yet.

I make my getaway, speed walking through the casino to the lobby, through the exit and out into a blast of dry heat, noise and commotion of the Strip. My pulse races as I sprint for the bus, making it just as the doors are closing, no plan in mind other than escape.

I don't know where I'm going.

Anywhere that isn't here.

2

Damian

Those legs, those eyes, those lips, those tits. Long, pale gold hair. I like brunettes just fine, but that shade of blonde does something to me.

Need, sudden and violent, rises within me as soon as her blue eyes lock with mine. The need to have her, to possess her. I don't know another woman who's made my cock this hard this fast. So I ask her name.

She brushes me off like a harmless mosquito who's landed for a quick bite. Not an experience I've had before.

Then she takes off while Dante and Cassio cackle and crack jokes at my expense. I lose sight of her for a few minutes as I join my brothers at the bar and I have no idea why I even care. But I do. I want to know where she is, who she is. I want to know every fucking thing about her.

"Blondie has reappeared," Dante says, as if I haven't already homed in on her like a fucking missile.

She stands across the casino floor beside a row of slot

machines. Even from this distance I notice two things: She looks scared and her right cheek is bright red. Like someone hit her. Fury ignites in my gut.

My gaze snares hers. Her eyes widen and she takes a half step toward me.

I feel a hand on my shoulder and turn my head toward my brother.

"Just heard from Dad," Cassio says, sliding his phone into the inside pocket of his jacket. "He wants to meet for dinner. Talk about the Ivanovs."

I grunt my assent and turn back toward the woman.

She's gone. Again.

"Fuck." I look around, but don't see her.

What I do see is a guy holding one hand to the side of his head, pushing through the crowd, going up on his toes and shifting side to side. Looking for someone. I've seen this guy before… Names don't always stick with me, but faces, I never forget.

I've seen that face more than once in the past few weeks. My hackles rise. I'm not a big believer in coincidence.

He notices me studying him and turns away. I follow his gaze toward the lobby and catch a glimpse of the woman.

"Dante, follow him. I want to know who he is and what he's doing here," I say, already walking away. People move out of my way on instinct. Cassio calls it the Red Sea effect.

The lobby's nearly empty when I get there. A group of older couples laughing and joking. Some people checking in. A lone guy talking loudly on his phone, as if he thinks the whole world is hanging on his every word.

No sign of the blonde.

I'm not sure why I feel disappointed. It's not like I can't get any piece of ass I want.

But for some reason, I want *her*.

We're in the private dining room at one of my father's favorite restaurants, the five of us at a table that can seat ten, Papa at the head, Leo at his right hand, facing the door, Dante beside him. I'm at Papa's left, facing the windows that overlook the garden, Cassio beside me. Sabina's going to be pissed that she wasn't included. My kid sister loves this place, but tonight is for business. I'll bring her a dessert to make it up to her.

The walls and drapery are deep royal purple; the overhead chandelier drips black crystals. Behind my father's chair is a large, ornate mirror that hangs above a credenza boasting silver-framed photos of famous—and infamous—guests. The feeling of the room is intimate, elegant.

An armed *soldato* stands just inside the closed door. There's another just outside. My father, Salvatore Russo, is a careful man.

"I don't like it, Papa," Leo says, frowning. He takes a sip of his Roagna Crichet Paje Barbaresco, a full bodied, dry red. It pairs well with pasta. Unfortunately for him, tonight the sixteen-course menu is French. Not a single pasta dish in sight. But Leo likes what he likes.

Papa savors a bite of Ossetra caviar, a sip of Sauvignon Blanc, glances at Leo, and shrugs. "Vlasta is dead. Mikhail is in charge. There is nothing to like or dislike."

Vlasta Ivanov died six months ago. Heart attack. He and Papa hadn't been friends. That would have been pushing it. But in our line of work, knowing your enemy is essential. There'd been a grudging respect between Papa and Vlasta and that meant our two families had been able to divide up Las Vegas in an amicable way.

Problem is, Vlasta's brother Mikhail inherited the leadership position, and Mikhail doesn't respect anyone. He's a wild card, and the way he's stomping on long held agreements is telling us we need a plan.

"He had a man at one of our casinos tonight," I say. We don't own the casino, but we do claim it as our turf. Despite a colorful history with organized crime, Las Vegas casinos are now owned and operated by large corporations, subject to rigid oversight and licensing. We can't directly get a finger in that pie. But while every casino has the occasional big winner, more often they have big losers. Our family's agreement with the Ivanovs means that we extend credit to the losers at our casinos and they extend credit at theirs. And by credit, I mean loans at two points a week. Some people might call that loan sharking. We call it business. "He's an Ivanov associate. I've seen him with Nikolai." Mikhail's son.

My father leans back in his chair. "What was he doing there?"

I play the scene in my mind. "Following a blonde."

Leo scowls. "You think Ivanov's running whores on our turf?"

I glare at him as Cassio lets out a hoot of laughter. "If she's a whore, she is the absolute worst at her job," he says. "She wouldn't even give Damian her name. Took off like he smelled like skunk and didn't even give him a backward glance."

"She is not a whore," I say, certain of that fact though I can't say why.

"Agreed," Dante says. "She was definitely personal."

"Still, one of Ivanov's men shouldn't have been anywhere near our place," Leo mutters, dark eyes flashing.

"You follow him?" I ask Dante.

"He didn't go far," Dante says. "He hung around, played the slots. Was still feeding a machine when I left to come here."

"You certain he works for the Ivanovs?" Cassio asks.

"Not certain," I say. "But I have a suspicion."

"Your suspicions are usually correct" Leo says. "What's he doing on our turf? What are the Ivanovs playing at?"

"We will meet with Mikhail," Papa says, his hands in motion as he speaks, emphasizing his words. "We will discuss, negotiate, come to an agreement." He grins at Leo and gently pats his cheek. "You worry too much, Leonardo."

Leo grits his teeth, then asks, "What if Mikhail doesn't want to discuss, negotiate, and come to an agreement? What if he wants what's ours?"

My father takes another bite, swallows, looks at me. "And you, Damiano? Dante? Cassio? You share your brother's concerns?"

That's Papa. Never favoring one child over the other. Always willing to hear opinions, weigh them before he makes a final decision.

"Mikhail's ruthless, which I can respect," I say, setting down my wine glass.

"But he's unpredictable," Dante says.

"Which makes him dangerous," Cassio says, pointing his fork at Dante to emphasize his point.

Papa reaches over and slaps Cassio's hand. "Manners," he says.

"Mikhail's dangerous even to his own," I say. Papa's

gaze lands on me. "There are rumblings that maybe Vlasta's heart attack was…encouraged by artificial means."

My father's expression sharpens. "You have proof?"

"Not yet," I say. "I'm working on it."

My father nods. Then his brows lower. His gaze scans the room.

The *soladata* by the door tenses.

Leo rises and turns a slow circle.

The hair on the back of my neck prickles and I glance at the door, then the windows. Something is off. We all feel it.

A shadow shifts outside the window.

I surge from my seat.

At the same time, I hear a sharp pop. The sound of glass breaking. Another pop.

I throw myself onto my father, sending his chair toppling back onto the floor, my body a shield over his.

Too late.

He lies on his back in the overturned chair, staring at the ceiling. There's a small, neat hole in his forehead. But the hole in the back of his head is neither neat nor small. Blood and brain and bits of bone cover my hands as I reach for the wound.

Bracing my weight on my right hand, I rear back and stare into my father's eyes. But he isn't there. He's gone, shot through the head and the heart with hollow-point bullets. Double tap.

His blood pools on the floor around my hand, warm and dark.

I'm dimly aware of Dante and Cassio tearing out of the room, going after the shooter, and of the two armed guards grabbing Leo and trying to drag him away. Protocol. The boss is dead. Protect the new boss.

Dead. My father is dead.
For a second, I feel nothing. Nothing at all.
And then pain and rage and hate flood my veins.
I throw back my head and howl.

3

Alina

Two months later

Emergencies only.

That's what I told Markus when I gave him my new phone number last week. And then I'd reiterated that I was being serious that he call me only if he had no other option. The night I'd fled the casino and Enzo had been a turning point for me. No more bad boys. And that included my brother. I love him. He's the only family I have left. But I can't let him bring his bad decisions into my life.

It's halfway through my shift when I feel my phone buzz in my apron pocket. It's an old phone, no screen, no call display, but I know it's Markus since he's the only one who has the number. I'd changed it the morning after Enzo hit me.

I quickly drop off a trayful of drinks at a table full of middle-aged businessmen, leering at me as if they fully believe I'll be the next one on stage, swinging around the pole with my tits and ass fully on display.

I'd be lying if I said I hadn't considered it—for half a second, anyway. Money's lean right now. I'd make a lot more of it working on the Strip, but this place, despite the scumbag clientele I've experienced since I started here, feels safer.

And I'm all about safety these days.

I'd originally taken the job waitressing at the Emerald—an off-Strip gentlemen's club—because I thought Enzo was less likely to find me here. But since the night he hit me, I haven't seen Enzo or a single face I recognize from my time with him, which I consider a very good thing. Maybe I'm being overly cautious, but I never want to see him again. Turns out that I might not need to worry. Enzo's disappeared. The night I'd taken off after he hit me was the last I've seen of him. Once I'd made it back to my tiny apartment, I'd double locked my door and hidden out for a week, but he never came after me. I still haven't heard from him. No call, no text, no explanation.

Gut instinct is telling me he's dead, that someone put a bullet in his head. Or worse.

Still, I'm lying low. He took me places—clubs, restaurants, a couple of parties. People saw us together. I'm connected to Enzo, which means I could be in danger. What if one of his associates thinks I know something valuable? I could swear I've felt someone watching me when I leave the club at night, but no matter how often I look around, I never see anyone. Maybe I'm paranoid. Maybe not. I would have left Vegas—*should* have left Vegas—but I don't have any money, and no family to fall back on. Just Markus.

And here we are.

By the time I lose the tray and grab the phone, it's stopped buzzing. At least, for all of five seconds before it starts again.

"I can't talk," is the first thing I say when I hold it to my ear.

"Hey, Sis," Markus says. "It's good to hear your voice."

I wish I could say the same. "I'm at work."

"I know. But I need you to do something for me."

I groan. "Markus, I said only emergencies—"

"This is an emergency," he cuts me off. "A big fucking emergency."

I finally hear the strain in his voice. It's usually covered really well by the bravado and easy confidence he slathers on like butter. Markus doesn't like to look weak to anyone. And he doesn't like to ask for help.

Unless it's a big fucking emergency.

Shit.

"What do you need me to do?" I ask.

He lets out a sigh then, a shaky, wavery sound that only ramps up my anxiety and concern.

"Go to my place. There's a spare key hidden in the cracked flowerpot to the left of the door. Under my bed is a black duffle bag. I need you to bring it to me."

"Should I ask why you can't go get it yourself?" I ask, voice tight.

"I'm a bit busy at the moment."

"Markus, what the fuck is going on?"

"Just…just do it. Please, Sis. Just do this one thing for me without a fuckton of questions, all right? Do this and I promise this is the last time I'll ask you for a favor like this."

I don't believe him. I've learned the hard way never to trust a drug addict with a gambling problem. I'd trusted him in high school when he told me he could double the money I'd saved from my part-time job flipping burgers. I never saw a penny of that money again. I'd trusted him my first year in college when he begged me to get him out of the hole he'd dug for himself. I'd given him what I could afford, and some I couldn't. He'd promised he'd pay me back, and he had…two years later. I'd had to take the graveyard shift at a gas bar to afford to eat for the rest of that semester. I'd trusted him when we each got a tiny inheritance after Mom and Dad died and he begged to borrow mine to pay off his debts, swore he'd pay me back every penny. He'd started out strong, sending money every month. Until he didn't. I'm still waiting for the rest.

"What casino are you at and how much do you owe?" I ask grudgingly.

"How the hell do you know I'm at a casino?"

I roll my eyes. "Let's call it a lucky guess."

He lets out another shuddery breath. "Like I said, this is the last time."

"Sure." I try to keep the sarcasm out of my voice, but it's a gift-with-purchase when it comes to being an audience member for a lifetime of Markus's issues. "Where are you?"

"Are you going to bring me the bag?" he presses.

"What happens if I say no? Got someone else to call in town that you trust?"

"Do you?" he asks softly.

My jaw tightens. "I asked first."

There's a grudging silence. We both know the answer to that. Neither one of us has anyone else in the world who gives a single shit about us. Anyone we can trust with our darkest secrets. It's a sad realization, but that doesn't make it any less true.

I wait. It doesn't take long before Markus tells me where he is.

I wave at Susan—the closest thing I have to a friend in Vegas—and gesture to let her know I'm leaving. She nods, mouths *call me later* and blows me a kiss, then points toward the boss's office, but I shake my head.

No sense trying to give some lame excuse to my boss about why I'm leaving early. He'll tell me I have to stay. So I just leave, knowing I'll have to find another dive to work at tomorrow.

It's okay, there are plenty of them in Vegas.

4

Alina

An hour later, black canvas duffle bag slung over my shoulder, I walk through the front entrance of the casino Markus directed me to. My heart's pounding hard, since it's smack-dab in the center of the Vegas Strip, swarming with tourists and thousands of pairs of eyeballs. I feel exposed, and it isn't just because my short black skirt and sequinned halter top leave little to the imagination. I might not be a stripper, but I'd quickly learned how to get maximum tips for minimal effort. I glance around, wondering if any of the people I pass are Enzo's associates.

Markus told me where to find him, so that's where I head. Through the casino, a distracting gauntlet of bells and dings from the slot machines, a low roar of conversation throughout the massive space, and shouts of glee or regret over the results at the blackjack and roulette tables. I ignore it all, focused only on my destination.

At the back is the entrance to the private VIP gaming rooms, and my steps slow when I see it's flanked by two hulking, musclebound guards wearing matching jet-black dress shirts and trousers. The monoliths eye me, expressionless.

"I'm here to see Markus Madsen," I tell them, raising my chin as I try to look like I did this sort of thing all the time. Totally confident, no problem at all.

Their gazes flick to the duffle bag and, without a change in his expression, one opens the door for me. I don't bother with a thank you before I swiftly move through it.

I've already decided not to do more than what I've been asked for. Find Markus, make sure he's all right. Give him the duffle bag. Then get the fuck out of here.

I can't let whatever shit Markus has gotten himself into tonight become my problem as well.

Past the entrance is a long, dimly lit hallway leading to an open door. Markus appears in the archway and quickly closes the distance between us. His light brown hair is disheveled, his shirt wrinkled. There are purple smudges under his blue eyes, and the scruff on his jaw is at least a couple of days old.

"I'm glad you're here," he says under his breath. "I wasn't sure you'd come."

"You weren't?"

"I'm never sure when it comes to you," he says.

His words sting since I'd like to think they're not the truth.

"The feeling's mutual." I shove the bag at him hard enough that he takes a step backward. Then I add, "Asshole."

This would usually earn me a grin, but not tonight. It worries me.

"Did you look inside?" he asks.

"No. I don't want to know what's inside." It's the truth, even though a million possibilities had gone through my mind on the way here.

"Good." Markus nods firmly. "Now, get out of here."

It's not like I expected a thank you. Or an excuse to get the fuck out of here at my earliest convenience. "Way ahead of you. Good luck with…whatever the hell this is."

Worry nags at me as I turn away, a bit reluctantly now, and take a few steps before I hear a deep, male voice that doesn't belong to my brother.

"Who are you?"

The sound freezes me in place. Three words, but I feel them twist right down to my core like hot silk.

I've heard those words before. That voice before.

Keep walking, I command myself. *And don't look back.*

But I can't move.

"She's my sister," Markus supplies when a deadly kind of silence falls over us.

"I didn't ask you," The Voice says. "I asked her."

I've often wondered what would have happened if I'd stayed right where I was that night when Damian Russo had asked my name. Or if I'd followed my impulse to run to him after Enzo had hit me.

I guess there's no time like the present.

"My name's Alina," I say, raising my chin as I finally turn to face him.

And there he is. My demon-angel.

No, not mine. Never mine. No more bad boys for me.

I note all the things I saw that night, and some I didn't. He's a little taller than Markus' six feet. Broad shoulders. Narrow hips. Lean muscle. He isn't wearing a suit tonight. Instead, he's wearing dark, slim fit jeans that outline muscular thighs and a dark gray casual button-down, open at the neck, sleeves rolled up to reveal forearms corded with muscle and covered in tattoos. His face is angular with high cheekbones and a straight nose. I stare at his lips as they shape my name.

"Alina," he repeats, sliding each syllable slowly over his tongue, like he's tasting it. Tasting *me*.

His gaze snares mine, those cold, dark eyes flaring with heat. I swallow. He's a forbidden fantasy come to life. Did he remember me? I give myself a mental shake. There's no way someone like Damian Russo would remember me. And I shouldn't want him to.

"She was just leaving," Markus says.

Damian tears his gaze from mine and glances at my brother. "Is that what you think?"

"Come on." Markus's voice is thin and reedy now. "She's not part of this."

One glance at Damian tells me my chance for escape tonight has come and gone. I'd blown a clean getaway.

"What the hell is going on here?" I ask.

"We're in the middle of a poker game," Damian says, and the edge of a smile turns up the corner of his mouth. It's a cruel smile.

Something inside of me goes cold.

I've heard about Damian Russo's infamous poker games. Again, that handy demon analogy fits nicely here. Rumor has it that he likes to win at any cost. That he has a taste for souls. Whatever someone cared about the most in this world, that was what he wanted to bet for. What he wanted to take. There'd been a couple of really drunk guys at the Emerald just last night talking about a friend of a friend that Damian Russo had destroyed.

Damn it, Markus, I think. *How the hell did you get into this mess with someone like him?*

"We're leaving," I say aloud as confidently as I can. "I need my brother's help with something super important. Come on Markus. Let's go."

"But we're not finished yet," Damian replies, before my brother can say anything. "Right, Markus?"

"Right," Markus replies with a mix of pain and regret in his voice.

"Then let's get on with it." Damian holds the door open and waits until Markus, without another glance at me, goes inside. Then Damian nods at me. "Join us."

"I'd really rather not—"

"I insist."

He says it smoothly, almost pleasantly. But this is not a negotiation. My heart pounds as I glance over my shoulder at the exit back to the main casino floor. Both of the musclebound guards are now standing on this side of the door, silently watching us.

"You need to know something about me, Alina," Damian says softly.

I hate that the sound of my name on his tongue makes things twist and tighten inside of me. "What's that?"

His gaze narrows. "I'm a man who expects to be obeyed."

I add that to my small dossier on Damian Russo.

Expects to be obeyed.

Son of Salvatore Russo, whose recent murder has been all over the news.

Brother of Leonardo Russo, the newly minted crime boss currently running Las Vegas.

A demon with a heart as black as his eyes, one who's

trapped Markus in a game that I know might mean the difference between life and death.

But that isn't all I know.

I also know I'll do anything it takes to save my brother.

5

Alina

"Put that on the table," Damian instructs, nodding at the duffle bag. Markus tosses it on the table. Two thugs stand off to one side. Damian gestures toward one of them, who draws closer, unzips the bag, and spreads it open.

Damian cocks his head. "Markus?"

I glance at my brother to see that his face has turned ghostly white.

"Alina?" My name is a strangled sound at the back of his throat.

"What?" I reply tensely.

"Where's the money?"

"What money?"

"Fuck," Markus whispers. He staggers closer to the duffle, reaching inside to frantically start pulling out a few pairs of balled up socks. Searching. "It was in here. All of it."

"What money?" I ask again, my voice strained. "Markus what the hell is going on here?"

He fishes out a navy T-shirt and stares at it like he'd

never seen anything so utterly disappointing in his life. "Fifty thousand."

I gape at him. "Fifty thousand dollars?"

He nods. "Part of what I owe."

"Only part of it?" My stomach lurches, then I force myself to look at Damian. He looks back at me, his expression ruthlessly neutral. "How much does he owe you?"

Damian's lips curve to the side. "I don't discuss business with just any—"

"How much?" I ask again, louder, and more forcefully.

His dark brow rises. "Sit down, Alina."

"I need to know—"

"Sit the fuck down," he says again, words as sharp as gunshots. "Now."

I'd sworn no one would ever boss me around or abuse me after what I'd endured from Enzo. I hadn't mourned him. His disappearance had frightened the hell out of me, but the thought that he was likely dead didn't bother me that much. I know admitting that makes me sound like a bad person, but so be it. It's the truth.

He'd been a bully who used violence to make him feel like a man.

But any fear I'd felt for Enzo paled in comparison to the terror of what only a few words from Damian Russo does to me.

The dark paneled walls of the private gaming room feel like they're closing in on me. I reluctantly sit down in the ivory upholstered chair next to the open duffle bag that seems to be filled with 100-percent my brother's clothes and zero-percent cash.

"Explain," Damian says to Markus.

Markus continues to stare bleakly at the navy T-shirt.

"This woman I've been with lately…Heather. She took off the other night after a big fight. This has to be her fault. No one else knew about the duffle."

"Alina did." Damian's voice is dangerously soft.

Markus' head snaps up. "Alina wouldn't have taken my money."

I feel Damian's gaze on me, searing and appraising. I force myself to meet it. I can't let him know he scares the shit out of me. "I don't steal."

"Everyone steals when they have the opportunity." His voice and expression are cold enough to send a shiver down my spine.

"I don't," I say again firmly. Then I look at Markus. "How much do you owe him?"

"Tonight? A hundred."

I know he's not talking about a hundred dollars.

"One hundred thousand," I say it out loud, and he flinches before nodding. I feel sick.

"I've been on a winning streak. That's how I got the fifty large. Tonight I was up for a while…" he begins.

"And then you weren't."

"And then I wasn't," he confirms grimly.

"How much in total if a hundred is just from tonight?"

It takes him several painful moments before he forces the word out. "Five."

Five hundred thousand dollars.

"Markus!" I suck in a deep breath to try to compose myself. I don't need to be an expert in stupidity to know owing half a million dollars to someone like Damian Russo isn't good for your health. "Okay, there has to be some way to fix this."

"There was." Damian nods at the duffle. "That was

supposed to be a down payment, but I'm afraid I can't take dirty laundry as collateral."

"I'll find Heather," Markus says, wringing his hands. "I can get you your money."

A devilish glimmer now sparks within Damian's dark eyes. He's enjoying this, the bastard.

"I have a better idea. How about we play another hand…and make it double or nothing for everything you owe me?"

"No," I say immediately, but it's muffled by Markus's enthusiastic "Yes!"

Like I said before, my brother is a gambling addict. And a certifiable dumbass.

Markus meets my pained gaze. "It's okay, Sis. Really. I've got this."

I ignore him and am now speaking directly to Damian. "Please don't do this. He's in deep enough as it is, and he clearly isn't thinking straight. There has to be another way to fix this."

Ignoring me as if I'm not even there, Damian sweeps the duffle off the table and dumps it on the floor as he takes a seat next to me. "Markus? Shall we?"

Desperation claws at me. "Markus," I whisper. My brother doesn't even glance my way.

The deck of cards is already in Damian's grip, and he shuffles them in one large, tattooed hand with ease. His gold and diamond watch, the same one he was wearing the first night I saw him, glints under the chandelier above the table.

Markus takes his seat, and something's changed in his demeanor. His eyes are shining, and a smile touches his lips. The prospect of winning the hand and canceling the entire debt he owes is exciting to him.

I can barely hear anything past the sound of my heart pounding in my chest.

Despite living in Vegas for months, I've never personally played a hand of poker, but I know the basics enough to realize that my brother has a bad poker face and far too much confidence given the shitty spot he's in. I can tell he's high too—or maybe drunk. Possibly both. Not a lot, just enough for it to cloud his already cloudy judgment.

Damian, on the other hand, seems stone cold sober and oozing confidence. The devil toying with a willing sacrifice just begging to be set on fire.

Cards are shuffled, dealt out. Markus looks at his briefly, then pushes three toward Damian. Damian deals three new cards to him, takes one for himself.

Time slows, every second feeling like a thousand.

A smile touches Markus lips as he turns his cards over.

Three tens. Not bad.

Damian barely looks at them before revealing three kings in his hand.

Better. Much better.

"I win," he says simply.

Double or nothing. In the span of a couple of minutes, Markus now owes Damian one million fucking dollars. The thought of it makes my stomach lurch. Then I almost laugh. How is owing a demon a million dollars any worse than owing him half a million? Both numbers are completely out of reach for my brother.

"Just where do you think he's going to get that kind of money?" I ask, and it's impossible to hide the fury in my words.

Markus says nothing, only staring at the cards in disbelief.

Damian glances at me. “If you can’t pay, you shouldn’t play.”

So true. But Damian had to have known before this game even began that my brother couldn’t pay. In fact, how had Markus even managed to buy a seat at the table with Damian Russo? They aren’t in the same universe, never mind the same league. None of this makes any sense.

“How do we know you didn’t cheat?” I ask, desperate for a way out, any way out. The venomous look that Damian fixes on me turns my blood to ice.

“I don’t fucking cheat,” he growls.

“Everyone cheats when they have the opportunity,” I say, parroting a version of his earlier assertion back at him.

Markus makes a choked sound, but I don’t look away as Damian stares at me in silence, then says, “I don’t.”

The way he looks at me makes me shiver, though I’m not sure if it’s fear or…something else.

“I guess I’ll have to take your word for it,” I say.

Damian gathers the cards with those long, strong fingers and sets the deck neatly to one side. “Your sister needs to show more respect, Markus.”

Fuck off, I think. And Damian meets my gaze directly, his eyes narrowed, as if he can read my mind.

“If you want respect, earn it,” I say.

Dark brows rise. Something flashes in his expression…amusement? Admiration? Annoyance? I can’t tell.

“I’ll get the money,” Markus blurts as he pushes up from the table, pulling Damian’s attention from me. “It’ll take me a little while, but I swear I can pay it. Come on, Alina. Let’s get out of here.”

The thugs step in front of the door as soon as

Markus makes a move in that direction. He casts a fearful look over his shoulder.

Damian crosses his arms over his chest and leans back in his chair.

"I'll get it. All of it." Markus just sounds desperate now. I don't think even he believes what he's saying.

"I know you will." Damian smiles, not a nice smile. White teeth and menace. "How long do you need?" he asks, so reasonable.

I rise from my chair, my legs shaky. Damian's sudden change in demeanor has me second-guessing my natural instincts now. Five minutes ago I would have bet that someone like him wouldn't let anyone walk away from a debt that high.

Markus's eyes rapidly shift as if he's doing calculations in his head. "A few months."

Damian chuckles darkly. "No. You have sixty days."

Markus inhales sharply. "Sixty days?"

"That's a generous offer, Markus. It's not ideal, but I'm willing to give you the time you need. It's a sizeable debt you owe me now."

My gaze moves to the expensive watch he wears. I'm not the biggest expert when it comes to luxury items, but I know it's easily worth a few hundred thousand. Damian doesn't need the money. He just likes to watch people squirm. He gets off on it.

"Double or nothing?" Markus says, laughing nervously. Then he flicks a sheepish look at me. "I'm kidding, of course."

"Why do I find that hard to believe?" I reply. There's this saying that when you are getting your way you should stop talking in case you mess it all up. Markus needs to stop fucking talking immediately.

"Sixty days to pay what you owe me in full," Damian says again. "Give me your word."

The word of an addict. Maybe Damian Russo isn't as smart as I thought.

Markus exhales in a rush. "You have it. Thank you, Damian. Really. Thank you." He turns to me. "Alina? Let's go. You can yell at me outside."

"Yelling is only the beginning of it," I mutter.

I take a step toward my brother, but Damian takes hold of my wrist to stop me. I look down with surprise. His touch is warm, strong, strangely electric. It's suddenly difficult to catch my breath.

"Alina will be staying with me," Damian says, his attention on my frowning brother.

"What?" I gasp. "No, I won't be doing anything of the sort."

Markus swears under his breath. "That's not necessary."

Damian rises, standing close by my side, his fingers still looped around my wrist. "Isn't it? You think I'm going to let you walk out of here just like that? Give you the chance to renege or disappear? Or try to, anyway. You owe me one million dollars, Markus."

"I…I can give you something else as collateral."

"What's that? Keys to your rented apartment? Your fifteen-year-old pickup truck? A couple dime bags of blow?" Damian turns to me and says, "Here's the way I usually do business. I extend credit at two points a week—"

"Points?" I ask.

"Percent," Damian says. I nod, trying to mentally calculate two percent of a million dollars, compounded weekly. "If I get paid, I make money. If I don't get paid, I seize assets and I make money. House. Car. Boat. Business. Jewelry. Doesn't matter to me. My goal is met either way. In the end, I make money." He gestures at my brother. "But Markus here has no assets. So he needs to provide collateral."

I guess Damian isn't willing to take the word of an addict after all.

He leans closer, his voice lowering. "I'm giving you a choice, Alina. You can walk out of here right now and I take my collateral from your brother in other ways." He sends a meaningful glance toward the two thugs by the door. "Or you choose to stay and your brother walks out of here untouched…for the moment. He gets sixty days to pay his debt and earn his way back into my good graces."

I swallow and whisper, "You want me to be a willing captive."

His gaze rakes me. "How much does family mean to you?" The last words are barely above a whisper, spoken so close that I feel his breath against my ear.

I close my eyes, sick, desperate. If I walk out of here, Damian will do something terrible to my brother. If I stay, he might do something terrible to me.

I think of all the times Markus has screwed me over.

Then I think of all the times he hasn't. I remember him buying me ice cream when we were kids and he only had enough money for one of us. I remember how he nursed me through the flu a week after we buried Mom and Dad. I remember Markus buying me pink ear protectors for my twelfth birthday because I was finally old enough to go to the Buffalo Rifle and Revolver Club with him and Dad.

I think about how his face lit up when I arrived on his doorstep here in Vegas. I sigh.

"Alina..." Markus says, and I don't know if he's begging me to stay or go. It doesn't matter.

"I'll stay," I whisper, fear coiling through me.

Damian turns to my brother. "You've got sixty days, Markus. Now get the fuck out of here before I change my mind."

He nods at his thugs who roughly escort Markus out of the room before my brother has the chance to say anything else. I watch with growing despair as the door closes between us.

I think I'd gone into shock while they had their brief and useless negotiation. But I finally find my voice.

"Let go of me," I snarl, yanking on my wrist.

Damian releases me. I realize his grip was never tight. There are no red marks on my skin. There will be no bruises tomorrow. He watches wryly, as if expecting me to make a break for it, but I stand my ground.

"I'll make this as simple as possible for you, Alina. If you attempt to run from me before your brother's debt is paid in full, then Markus will pay for your mistake with much more than money," he tells me, his tone flat and matter of fact. "Do you understand me?"

I'd already guessed that outcome all by myself. "So I'm your prisoner now."

"You're my guest. For sixty days."

"I have a life. Friends." It's mostly a lie, but he doesn't have to know that. "I can't just leave it all behind with no notice."

"Yes, you can." He pauses. "You walked out of the Emerald mid-shift without even letting your boss know. You don't have a job there to go back to. Your furnished apartment is month to month, and the month renews in three days. Your landlady won't miss you. As for friends, you occasionally grab a drink with a girl from work. I believe her name is Susan. You haven't stayed in touch with people from high school and your closest friend from college is in the UK doing a Masters in Architecture."

I gape at him. How can he know so much about me, a person whose name he didn't even know an hour ago? I think about all the times in recent weeks that I felt like someone was watching me and I shiver.

"This is insane," I say. "You're insane. You can't just control people like this. Force them to do what you want."

"Can't I?" He watches me, almost amused. Like a cat observing a mouse begging not to become tonight's dinner.

"What happens if Markus can't pay you what he owes on time?" I ask, hating the weakness I hear in my own damn voice.

Damian takes hold of my chin and forces me to meet his gaze. "If he can't pay, I'll take something else of value. I'll get my money's worth, one way or the other. Accept this, Alina. You have no choice in the matter. For the next sixty days, you belong to me."

6

Damian

THERE ARE three things I believe in: Family. Fortune. And fucking.

Alina Madsen chose family, chose to stay in order to keep her brother safe. That kind of loyalty is something I can respect. Family is everything.

I study her for a second, the pale blond fall of her hair, the proud tilt of her head, the blue eyes that watch me warily. After tonight, I might consider adding a fourth F.

Fate.

I've never believed in it before. But maybe I do now.

As I'd knelt beside my father, his blood and brains smearing my hands, I'd sworn to find his killer, to make the bastard pay. Blood for blood. Bone for bone.

But in order to kill the killer, I need to find him first.

Leo was immediately pulled into running the business. As much as he wanted to focus every moment on finding my father's murderer, he's been groomed since childhood to step in as boss. So that's what he did. He sent Dante to New York and Cassio to Chicago to deal with business there while I spoke with informants, followed up on the tiniest lead, watched security tapes for hours, days, searching for some hint that might identify the shooter. There hadn't been anything to find. It had been a professional hit. The guy had been smart. Careful. I went back and watched the tape from a day before the shooting. Then two days. Then three. And for a split second, I saw a blurry, grainy face I recognized.

An hour later, I had his name.

Enzo Bianchi. 32 years old. Born and raised in New York City until he moved to Vegas last year. That, literally, was all the information I could find on him, even with my sources who can usually uncover nearly anyone's deepest darkest secrets.

I'd seen Bianchi before. Not just at the casino with Alina, but other times, too. And I realize now that other than the night at the casino, each of those times was when I was with my father.

At the very least, Bianchi knows something about my father's murder. Quite possibly, he is the killer. Either way, he's a dead man, but only after he screams and begs for mercy as I flay the skin from his living body. Only after I confirm my suspicion that he was acting on orders from Mikhail Ivanov.

Problem is, Bianchi has disappeared.

So I followed the only lead I had. I sent my people to find out everything they could about the blonde he had been with the night my father was shot.

No, that's not the entire truth. I would have sent my people to find her even if she'd had nothing to do with Bianchi. She's been living in my head rent-free for two months. I don't usually spare a thought for a woman I've fucked, never mind one I haven't. Maybe my fixation is some sort of penance, some sort of guilt over not rescuing the damsel in distress. If I'd rescued her that night, I'd have killed Bianchi before he had the chance to kill my father.

But the white knight thing isn't my style. I don't rescue people. I'm the one people beg to be rescued from.

My people had no trouble tracking her down. They've been watching her, expecting that Bianchi would get in touch. But she's had no contact with him. In fact, based on her behavior—she changed her phone number, moved out of her shitty apartment and into an even shittier one, got a new job—I'd say she's studiously trying to avoid contact. Hiding from him.

Still, she might know something.

I considered having her picked up, questioned. It turned out that fate had a better plan.

Fate delivered Markus Madsen—a guy who's done a few jobs for the family—straight into my hands. He reached too high and bought into a game he shouldn't have. My game.

Markus Madsen, brother of Alina Madsen, the woman who might be the key to finding my father's killer.

The woman I fuck every night in my fantasies.

I'm the type to take advantage of the perfect opportunity, no matter who it hurts.

If I'd had my people pick Alina up, I'd have spooked Bianchi before he reached out to her. If I had my people question her, she might have given me the information I want. Or she might have protected Bianchi. Hard to know.

Now Alina's focus is on Markus. She'll be so worried about her brother, she won't think to guard any information she might have about Bianchi. Alternatively, she'll offer up everything she knows in order to buy her brother's freedom. And the icing on the cake? Bianchi will hear that I have her and he'll wonder exactly what secrets she's spilling. That might make the rat slink out of his hidey hole.

But honesty makes me acknowledge that there's another reason I didn't have my people question her.

From the second I first saw her, the primal, primitive, reptilian part of my brain has screamed *mine*.

If she has answers, I'll be the one to pull them from her lush, soft lips.

"Let's go," I say with a nod at Vito and Joe. Then I turn to Alina and make a sweeping gesture for her to precede me. "Ladies first."

She shoots me a look, venom in her blue eyes. If she had a knife, she'd stab me. I'd like her to try. I'd like to pin her underneath me and hold her while she squirms.

"Such a gentleman." Her words drip sarcasm.

I shrug. "Not really. I just want to stare at your very fine ass in that very short, very ugly skirt." Her eyes widen. "Now move," I say, my tone hard.

She moves, walking ahead of me and fuck me but her ass is perfection. Nice and round. It pisses me off that she's wearing a polyester skirt with an uneven hem and a cheap sequined top. Those legs, those tits, they should be showcased in silk. Or showcased in nothing but stiletto heels and a band of diamonds that I put around her delicate neck.

As if she can hear my thoughts, she glances back at me over her shoulder. Her eyes hold mine for an instant and then she quickly looks away.

I TAKE HER TO THE PENTHOUSE ON LAS VEGAS BLVD., one of several properties we own in the city. We pull into the underground. Park. Vito and Joe exit the vehicle, alert for any threat. I get out and walk around to open Alina's door, positioning myself directly in her path. I don't move away as she swings her legs to the side, or as she straightens, her breasts just inches from my chest.

She tips her head back to look up at me. "You going to move?" she asks. *Asshole*, I can see her add silently.

"Such a smart mouth. Maybe I should put something in it to keep you quiet." I step back just enough to let her pass.

"My teeth are sharp. Little rabbit teeth. And I like to bite," she says, the slight waver in her tone telling me this is all bravado.

I catch her hand, pulling her to a stop, my chest against her back, her ass pressed against my cock. She freezes.

I take my time running my palm along the side of her waist, her hip, the swell of her ass. Then I lean in and say softly against her ear, "Biting will get you punished." She sucks in a breath. "I'll spank those round cheeks until they're a pretty shade of pink, all flushed and hot from my hand. Then I'll fuck you, nice and slow, take my time while you beg me to let you come. Maybe I'll slide a finger in your ass…"

She makes a strangled sound and spins to face me. Her pupils are wide and dark, her irises a thin line of blue. Her lips part. Her breath comes a little faster. The tip of her tongue darts out to wet her lips. She's afraid of me. And she wants me. It's a combination that's alluring as hell. A little fear can be a lot of fun.

Her eyes narrow. She presses those lush lips together. And then her heel slams down on my instep.

"Fuck you," she says and stalks toward the open door of the elevator that's currently flanked by Vito and Joe.

I catch her in two strides and walk with her to the elevator where she moves to the opposite corner, as far from me as she can get. I insert the card that allows access to the penthouse. The elevator opens into a marble foyer with double doors opposite us. There are no other doors in this foyer; this is a private floor.

She pauses when we enter the condo, gasping when she sees the view. Lights and night sky and the Sphere, currently aglow in shades of blue and violet. The entire wall is floor to ceiling windows behind a massive white u-shaped sectional. To the left of the couch is a gas fireplace set in a wall of white marble. To the right is a live edge acacia wood dining table surrounded by mid-century modern white chairs and beyond that, a state-of-the-art kitchen complete with a six-burner stove and an island as big as a football field.

"This is where you'll be staying," I say. "As my guest."

"Guests are allowed to leave. Am I?" she asks, her tone flat.

"Not yet." I nearly smile at the death glare that earns me. Then I hold out my hand. "Phone."

"What?"

"Give me your phone."

"No. I'm not going to give you—"

I rest my index finger against her lips. They're soft and smooth. I wonder if she'll try to bite me. I'm almost disappointed when she doesn't. "Give it to me or I will take it. And you will be punished for not obeying me."

She shakes her head. "I need to know that my brother's okay. That's why I want my phone."

"I'll be in touch with Markus. I'll give him your regards."

Her tough façade cracks, her expression growing desperate. Her eyes are blazing but they're moist, like she's fighting tears. "I love my brother, but he's a fuck up. He's gotten himself into a mess he can't fix all by himself. He needs me."

In my business, the difference between living and dying can depend on spotting a lie. I'm very good at it. And Alina is not lying. She's terrified for her brother and she honestly believes she can get him out of this.

"Markus is more resourceful than you think he is," I say. "This is a good challenge for him. It's only a million dollars."

She scoffs. "You're out of touch with reality. You don't think a million is a lot? It is. It's the kind of money that can change lives."

"Or destroy them," I add.

"You get off on this, don't you? Walking around in your ten-thousand-dollar suit, flashing your offensively expensive watch, being driven around in your shiny black sedan. Luring victims into your little trap for your own amusement. It's disgusting. You're disgusting."

"Be careful what you say to me, Alina."

"Or what?" The words are a challenge, but her tone is a breathy whisper.

I close the distance between us, threading her golden hair between my fingers, wrapping it around my wrist, giving a little tug. Not tight enough to hurt—not yet—but more than tight enough to get her attention. She inhales sharply, her chest expands, and her breasts press against the thin material of her shirt. Her nipples are hard pebbles.

"Or what?" I repeat, my mouth close to hers.

She's panting, her breath fanning my lips.

And I've had enough of this game. With a growl, I claim her mouth, hard and insistent, my tongue tasting her, twining with hers. She freezes, not moving, not breathing. Then she makes a delicious sound of submission, of need, and she melts against me as I take what I want.

Fuck, she's hot. So damn hot.

I pull on her hair, making her head tip back, giving me access to her pale throat. I run my tongue down the line of muscle, then close my teeth on her skin, marking her.

From the second I saw her, I had the urge to possess her.

What the fuck is it about this woman?

The primitive beast inside me roars, *mine.*

7

Alina

I FEEL the sting of Damian's teeth on my throat, then the soft swipe of his tongue, soothing the hurt. My head spins. My pulse pounds. I've never been this turned on in my life. And just from a kiss. A single feral, forbidden kiss.

I twine my fingers through his dark hair as his mouth finds mine again. God, he can kiss. Hot and deep and hungry.

I hear the sound of the front door closing. Who—?

The thugs. Vito. Joe. Were they standing there watching us?

Through my lust induced fog, sanity claws its way forward.

What the hell am I thinking? I'm already the queen of dumb-ass choices. But fucking Damian Russo an hour after he takes me prisoner would make me the empress of idiocy.

With a groan, I try to pull away. He still has my hair wrapped around his fist, his other arm a solid band around my waist, holding me up. My legs are like rubber.

His lips are on mine, insistent, demanding, and I almost give in, almost sink into the heat and power and need.

No. No. Stop, I tell myself. *I'm stronger than this. Smarter than this. No more bad boys for me. Ever.*

"No." I manage to force that single word out.

And to my surprise, he stills instantly, rearing back to look down at me.

One dark brow lifts. "You fucking loved every second of that," he says.

"That doesn't mean I'm stupid enough to—" I break off with a shake of my head, trying to pull free of his hold on my hair. "Let me go."

That gorgeous, carnal mouth curls in a dangerous smile.

"Not for sixty days," he says. Then holds out his hand, palm up. "Phone."

I stare at him, angry, embarrassed, confused. Then I slap my phone against his palm.

He offers a low laugh as he studies my expression. "If this kitten had claws, I'd be bleeding from a dozen places."

He steps away as if that kiss meant nothing at all, as if he didn't feel what I felt. Everything about this situation is out of my depth, so I fall back on my old standard and say, "Fuck off."

"Sleep tight, Alina," he says with a knowing grin, then turns and leaves without looking back.

I WRAP MY ARMS AROUND MYSELF, FEELING COLD.

For lack of anything else to do, I go to the kitchen and check the fridge. Bottled water. Two cans of soda. No food.

The cupboards are equally bare, except for a tin of smoked oysters, a box of cheddar crackers, and a huge hazelnut milk chocolate bar in gold wrap. I can make a meal out of that.

The wine fridge is fully stocked, as is the bar in the living room. Clearly, Damian has his priorities.

I wander through the rest of the condo. There's a bedroom and ensuite bathroom at one end of the vast living space and a second bedroom with ensuite at the other. Soaker tub. Walk-in shower. No expense spared. My entire apartment would fit into just one of those bathrooms. The décor in each bedroom is identical, with California king beds, chic side tables, lamps, a dresser, and a small sofa with coffee table. No knick-knacks. No photos. No clothes in the drawers or the huge walk-in closets.

This isn't Damian's home. This is a spare location to stash his victims. Or one-night stands.

Or hell, both.

Unfortunately, there are also no phones.

When I come out of the bedroom, I stifle a squeak of surprise.

There's a good-looking guy sitting on the huge sectional. He's reading a book. He glances at me.

"Hi there," he says.

"Hi," I reply uneasily.

"You're Alina."

"That's…me. Yes. Who are you?"

"I'm Luca."

I nod slowly. "Luca," I repeat. "And let me guess. You work for Damian Russo."

"I prefer to say that I work *with* him. But, sure. Either works."

"He's keeping me here against my will."

"You're free to leave whenever you like."

My eyes widen. "I am?"

Luca puts his book down on his lap so he can gesture toward the door. "I mean, I'll be accompanying you, but still. Feel free to go for a walk. You're not a prisoner. You're Damian's guest."

"I'm his guest, am I?" I say with scorn. "Is that what he told you?"

Luca stands up, carelessly tossing the book on the couch. With shock I realize that it's one of the Harry Potter novels. He notices my scrutiny and shrugs.

"Those books helped to get me through a rough time in my teens. I'm rereading them out of nostalgia. The movies, while good, just aren't as good as the books."

"I didn't ask."

Luca smirks. He has that smug look that only very handsome, very confident men can pull off. "Don't worry, I get the attitude. I know this is not an ideal situation for anyone, but it is what it is. Do you want to go out somewhere?"

"With you breathing down my neck," I say.

"That's right."

When Luca gets closer to me, I realize how tall and heavily muscled he is. And while his voice is friendly enough, there's a menacing quality to his hazel eyes. An underlying warning to toe the line.

"No. I'm fine."

"Glad to hear it. Now, if it's okay with you, I'm going to get back to my book."

"You do that."

He turns and I notice the weapon at the small of his back. 6 o'clock carry. A Glock 17. It's a fairly big gun, but he's a big guy. It's a reminder that he isn't harmless, that for all his assertions that I'm a guest, I'm actually a prisoner held here by an armed guard, and that my brother's life hangs in the balance.

Unsettled, I go back to the bedroom I've decided to claim as my own, walking right across the large space to the balcony doors. Out on the balcony, there's a fantastic—no, breathtaking—view of Vegas. All sparkling lights and humming energy that is hard to explain except to say that this is a town where people come to have fun and sometimes get into trouble.

I haven't experienced much of the fun yet, but I've had more than my share of trouble.

Being alone with my thoughts for too long isn't a good idea because I start to play Choose Your Own Adventure with how this could go down. If Markus doesn't manage to pull a million dollars out of his ass in two months, what then? Is he…killed? How does a man like Damian Russo deal with someone who owes him money except with violence?

And what happens to me then?

Anxiety gnaws at me.

No. I won't let myself spiral like this. I'm a smart girl. I can figure out how to save my own neck and Markus's too. I just wish I could talk to my brother, try to come up with a plan of action. Luca says he's not here to keep me from escaping, but of course that's exactly why he's here. I'm a prisoner.

And if I do manage to escape, they'll expect me to go straight to Markus, which will make it easy for me to be returned to my luxurious prison. And if I don't go find

Markus? If I take off on a bus to anywhere? Then my brother is completely on his own, and I doubt Damian will honor the two-month time frame. Markus will be out of time.

I WAKE UP WITH DAYLIGHT STREAMING IN THROUGH THE floor to ceiling windows. My body is humming, alive, electric. I think I must have been having a really hot dream, one featuring a demon-angel who kissed me like he owned me…

It takes me a moment to remember where I am, but when I do, I'm on my feet so quickly that I get dizzy.

I look around the room. Something's different. There are several cardboard boxes piled up next to the door. I approach them tentatively and slowly open the one on the top, shocked to see they're filled with my belongings—clothes, shoes, makeup, toiletries. It looks like the sum total of everything I had in my shitty little apartment. Someone came into this room and put those there and I slept right through it.

Damian Russo's been to my home. He knows where I live.

And he packed everything I own up and brought it here.

The thought of him—or one of his thugs—riffling through my personal belongings and throwing it all in boxes pisses me off. It takes a minute before I calm down. I suppose I could pitch a fit, make myself a nuisance for every single day I'm stuck here.

But I know that's not the right plan.

Someone like Damian would expect others to obey his commands without question. I have no power here.

No matter how hard I fight, how much I scream or try to talk my way out of this, nothing is going to change until Markus makes good on his debt. If anything, I know it could get even worse. Much worse.

So the plan is to be nice, even if I have to grit my teeth to do it.

I will say "thank you for bringing me my belongings," instead of "who gives you the fucking right to go to my apartment and touch my shit without permission?"

Men like Damian Russo don't ask for permission. And they'd never ask for forgiveness.

I spend twenty minutes putting my things away in the closet and drawers. Then I take a long hot shower before picking out fresh clothes to wear. I even take extra time with my hair and make-up, so I'll look less like a screaming banshee and more like a reasonable, business-minded sister concerned only for her brother's future wellbeing.

It's a plan. I never said it's a great plan, but I'll improvise where necessary.

I've worked out all the potential scenarios that today can bring, and suddenly come to the realization that Damian might not even step foot in here again for sixty days. Why would he? I'm safely holed away in this lush prison with Luca babysitting me until further notice.

That potential outcome is dismissed the moment I open the bedroom door and see Damian sitting at the long dining table, facing me. As if he's been waiting for me to emerge.

His gaze travels slowly down my body then slides back up to my face, pausing for a split second on the mark he left on my neck. I feel that look as if he's touched me and suddenly all I can think of are the things he said he wanted to do to me, the feel of his arms around me and his mouth on mine, the hard ridge of his cock pressed against me. I am not usually this horny or this stupid. Maybe Damian Russo put something in the water.

8

Alina

"Good morning," I say, trying to force aside the memories of Damian kissing me, touching me, marking my skin. I dreamed about him last night and woke up with my body thrumming like a live wire. Ugh. I don't want to dream about him, don't want to want him. Sucks that my body doesn't care what my brain wants.

"I've ordered breakfast," he says, his voice like smooth, dark silk. He's wearing faded jeans, worn and soft, and a black t-shirt, the short sleeves pulled taut by the bulge of his biceps, the material stretching across his shoulders and chest, hanging a little loose at his waist. "It should be here any minute now."

"Oh. Okay." I wet my lips.

He's silent for a moment, and then, "Let's talk, Alina."

"Talk? About what?" Nervousness swarms over me like I've accidentally stepped on a nest of ants.

Damian nods at the chair to his right. "Take a seat."

I want to resist, but I do what he tells me to do, reminding myself of the plan to be nice and the fact that he has made it clear he expects to be obeyed. I sit, fighting to keep my expression calm.

"Did you sleep well?" he asks.

"Well enough. I was surprised to find my all my things here this morning. More surprised that their delivery didn't wake me up." I manage to keep any animosity out of my tone.

"It wasn't me. After I arrived this morning, I sent Luca to collect your things."

Damian must have been here very early this morning if Luca had enough time to collect and pack all my shit.

"He tells me you've met," Damian says.

"Briefly last night. Enough to know he's a Harry Potter fan."

"Is he?"

I nod, and this is the moment that the front door opens and the six-foot-five Potterhead in question enters the condo, carrying a large paper bag and a tray with two coffees.

Damian's attention doesn't leave me for a moment. I feel the heat of his gaze on me as I watch Luca place the bag on the counter, pull out a bunch of white take-away containers and set them on the table along with the tray of coffees. He collects dishes from a cupboard and cutlery from a drawer.

"Bon Appetit," he says dryly before leaving us alone again.

My stomach grumbles with hunger, since I literally don't remember the last meal I had. Something quick and forgettable for lunch yesterday. I never ended up eating the crackers and chocolate last night.

Damian pushes a coffee toward me and takes one for himself. "Latte. Extra hot. Extra foam. One shot caramel syrup, one shot vanilla syrup. Cinnamon sprinkled on top," he says.

He knows my weirdly specific coffee order. I find that unsettling.

I find everything about him unsettling.

"Eat something," he tells me.

His commanding tone pisses me off. "No thank you. I'm not hungry."

He opens the containers to reveal scrambled eggs, bacon and sausage, fruit cocktail, French toast, and chocolate croissants, which are my favorites. He takes a plate and piles food onto it, everything except a croissant. I have the crazy thought that he got them for me. How would he know that I like them?

The same way he knows so many other things about me, including how I like my coffee.

I have a feeling that Damian Russo can find out anything and everything if he sets his mind to it.

I study him, trying to keep a neutral expression on my face. My stomach complains again and I'm sure he can hear it, even though he doesn't say anything.

He starts to eat, still watching me with narrowed eyes.

Maybe one piece of bacon won't matter…

I clasp my hands together on my lap and try to think about something else to say.

"Where's my brother?" I ask.

He takes his time answering. "I don't know."

"Is he safe?"

"I don't know."

I swallow down a snarky comeback to that infuriating response. Or lack of response.

"Is this why you're here?" I ask, nodding at his plate of food. "For breakfast?"

"Partially. The food at this restaurant is particularly good."

My stomach chooses that moment to growl.

"I told you to eat. You refused," he says, his tone silky, laced with steel. "I am not in the habit of repeating myself, but I am making an exception and telling you again, eat. It is not a request."

I'm a man who expects to be obeyed.

I almost argue just for the sake of arguing, but fuck it. What am I trying to prove? I grab a plate and load it up.

I bite into the croissant. The buttery, flakey, chocolatey goodness almost makes me cry. He watches me chew and swallow, his eyes on my lips. I feel my cheeks heat. He grins like he won a prize. An open, honest grin that makes my heart twist in my chest. White teeth. Tiny crinkles at the corners of his eyes. For an instant, he isn't a deadly criminal, he's just an insanely hot guy sharing a smile.

"We weren't formally introduced last night," he says. "Do you know who I am?"

"I know who you are," I reply, and leave it at that. Or I try to, anyway.

"Okay, so tell me. Who am I?" His deep voice is casual as he takes a sip of his coffee.

"Damian Russo."

"That's my name. Yes. But who am I?"

Mafia prince. Criminal. Villain. Killer.

Of course, I don't say this out loud.

"You're someone who likes scrambled eggs," I tell him. "And playing poker. Actually, no. *Winning* poker."

"Both are correct." Damian takes another bite of food, chews thoughtfully, and swallows. "Do you know who my father was?"

Did I imagine his voice catching on the word *father*?

"I do," I admit. "Salvatore Russo."

"And who was he?"

"A man with a lot of power here in Vegas," I reply carefully. "He owned a lot of property. Businesses. I think he had something to do with construction and waste management." At least, that's what the news claims. The news also mentioned money laundering, extortion, and sports betting. There were articles that mentioned his children—Leonardo, Damiano, Dante, Cassio, and Sabina—and the fact that his wife is deceased. But mostly, the news has focused on his murder.

I know what it feels like to lose both parents. I know the heartbreak, the pain, the feeling of being lost, adrift. My own grief wells as I whisper, "My condolences on your loss. And to your brothers. And your sister."

Damian's fork freezes halfway to his mouth and his gaze flicks to me. Something slides behind his dark eyes, a sliver of pain. A glimpse at a deeper well of grief. But it's gone in an instant, replaced with something harder. He puts down the cutlery and places his hands on either side of his plate.

"Markus is the only family I have left," I say into the silence. For this frozen second, we're both orphans, our parents gone. We both know what it feels like to only have our siblings.

"What happened to your parents?" he asks.

I think he already knows what I'm going to say, but I answer anyway. "Both are dead. Car accident." I shake my head. "I hate that word. Accident means unexpected and unintentional. It wasn't an accident. It was a man who chose to drive drunk. Who chose to kill them."

He leans forward, his gaze intent, holding mine. "And you would have liked to see him pay."

"I..." I swallow, seconds ticking past. I've never admitted this before, not out loud. But something about Damian's expression, something about the fact that he understands what it feels like makes me say, "Yes. He got off with a slap on the wrist even though he'd been caught driving drunk before, more than once. My parents' lives should have been worth...more."

Still he doesn't look away. "Did you want to see him suffer? See him dead?"

There's something about Damian's expression, the intensity, the genuine understanding, that pulls the truth from me. I hesitate, then go all in. "Yes. I wanted to see him suffer. See him dead. I still do." For the first time since Mom and Dad died, I say it out loud, because somehow, I feel like I can, like Damian Russo will understand. Like he won't judge me. And how crazy is that? Why should I care if a criminal judges me?

"Sometimes, I imagine terrible things happening to him." I roll my suddenly dry lips inward, swipe my tongue across them. Then I tell him the worst part. "Sometimes, I imagine that *I* do terrible things to him."

"Payback," he says with a small smile.

"Payback," I whisper. I can't believe I told him this. I've never said this to anyone, not even Markus.

"I understand," he says.

I nod. He understands. He does. I have no doubt that he wants to do terrible things to the man who shot his father.

What does it say about me that I get it, that I don't think he's wrong?

He leans back in his chair, steepling his fingers. Long, strong fingers. The backs of his hands decorated with tattoos that trail up his arms and disappear beneath his t-shirt. He looks just as good in casual clothes as he did in a suit. I have the crazy urge to trace the lines of those tattoos with the tip of my finger.

"What about your boyfriend?" he asks.

That question breaks the gossamer thread that joined us.

"I don't have a boyfriend. No pets. No dog, or cat, or even a goldfish. Just an older brother who's in over his head with the wrong man and managed to drag me into the center of his problems without any warning."

I literally bite my tongue to stop me from talking since my tone has become anything but amiable. But I'm angry. For a second, I forgot that this man is holding me in a luxurious prison. For a second, I actually liked him, trusted him with my secrets. And then he brought me crashing back to reality. So I'm angry at myself. At him. I can't let myself forget who this man in front of me is. My jailor. The man who holds my brother's safety—hell, my brother's life—in his hands.

"Do you know how my father died?" Damian asks. "You would have seen it in the papers, in the news."

I lick my suddenly dry lips. "He was shot."

"Two bullets. Hollow-points. They're designed to expand on impact, to do as much damage as possible. One got him here." He leans toward me and rests his fingers on the swell of my left breast, over my heart. My breath locks in my throat. "And one here." He taps the tip of his index finger on the center of my forehead. I shiver.

"I was as close to him then as I am to you right now," he says, his gaze locked on mine. "I can still feel my father's blood, his brains, on my hands."

I feel the color drain from my face. "That…that's truly horrifying. I'm so sorry."

I don't care who Damian is, I wouldn't wish a traumatic experience like that on my worst enemy.

"That day I made a promise. To myself, to my brothers. My sister. I promised that I would find the shooter."

And make him suffer, he doesn't say. But I hear it anyway, and I understand.

"I think you can help me, Alina," he says.

His words take me by surprise. "You think *I* can help you?"

He nods.

"How?" I ask.

He slides his phone across the table. I glance down at the screen, at the photo there, and for a second, I'm just confused. And then I'm wary.

"That's your boyfriend," Damian says. "Enzo Bianchi."

He doesn't pose this as a question.

It is a picture of Enzo. Not clear at all, quite blurry. Taken from a distance. But it's definitely him.

"Not my boyfriend," I correct, uneasily. "I haven't seen him in a while."

I can't tell if he believes me or not.

"How long exactly?" Damian asks.

I tear my gaze away from the screen. My heart is pounding hard as a million memories of my abusive ex rise up in my mind. I push the phone away from me.

"I…I don't know. A couple months?" I'm lying. I know exactly how long it's been. The last time I saw Enzo was the first time I saw Damian Russo. The night Damian's father was shot.

My eyes widen. "Wait. You think Enzo killed your father."

He takes his phone back. "Where is he?"

"I don't know. One day, he just wasn't there anymore. He didn't explain, he just disappeared."

"You didn't go looking for him?"

"No."

"Why not?"

"Because I was glad he was gone."

Damian sits with this for a moment. "I want to find him."

"I'm sure you do. But I don't know where he is."

"I don't fucking believe you."

"That's too bad, because it's the truth."

He hisses out an impatient sigh. "Who did Enzo work for?"

"I don't know." Another lie. I'd overheard snippets of conversations, enough to know Enzo unofficially—or maybe officially—worked for the Ivanovs. I'm not sure why I don't just tell Damian the truth. But my sense of self-preservation is strong and so I hold back that bit of information in case I need it later.

He cocks his head, his expression one of impatience now. "How long were you together?"

"A couple of months. And we weren't exactly together. He took me out sometimes."

He reaches over and strokes the backs of his fingers along my right cheek. I fight the urge to lean into his touch. "He hit you."

"How do you know—?" I remember the impulse I had to run to him that night, to seek protection from Enzo. I take a slow breath. "Yeah. He hit me."

Damian's expression has gone cold. "Often?"

I shake my head. "He hit the wall. Yelled a lot. Yanked me around by the arm. Left bruises. I was done. I met him one last time to tell him that. That's the night he hit me…"

"You broke up with him before he disappeared."

"Yes. And I haven't heard from him since. For all I know, he's dead."

"What makes you say that, Alina? Did he do something that would get him killed?" His voice is low, his tone easy, the sort of tone that invites confessions.

I swallow and wrap my arms around myself. "It's a figure of speech."

"Who did he work for?"

"I don't know," I say again, louder this time. I'm not protecting Enzo. I'm protecting myself. And Markus. Information is power and I'm not going to give it away now in case I need it later. "But I do know that he did things. Bad things."

"Bad things," he repeats, a hard smile curving his lips. "Like what?"

"I don't know."

"Those are your favorite three words, aren't they?" Damian stands up and comes toward me, pulling a chair next to me. It scrapes along the floor with the subtlety of nails on a chalkboard. He sits, so close I can smell the faint citrus and spice scent of his skin. "I need answers, Alina."

"Here are your answers. I dated Enzo for a couple of months. He was an asshole. Sometimes, I didn't see him for days. Once, I didn't see or hear from him for a week. A couple of times, he was all scraped up when I saw him, his knuckles split. If I asked him any questions, he liked to yell at me or shake me until I shut the hell up. I learned pretty quickly not to ask any questions."

Fury flashes in his dark eyes.

"When I find him, I'm going to fucking kill him," he mutters, and then grasps hold of my chin to make me meet his gaze when I look away. "I'm going to make him suffer. Do you hear me?"

"Be my guest," I snarl. "But I still don't know where he is."

He doesn't let go of me. His hold is gentle, his skin warm. His attention moves briefly to my lips, then flicks back up to my eyes.

"He hit you that night at the casino." Not a question, but I nod anyway.

"Because you ended it?"

"No."

"Why, then?"

"Because I was talking to you," I say. "Or, well, because you were talking to me."

A frown creases his forehead. "I asked your name. You didn't give it to me. That's all it took?"

"No. I think it was the way you were looking at me."

"How was I looking at you?"

"Like you wanted to fuck me." I regret saying this the moment the words leave my mouth. "That's what Enzo said, anyway."

Damian's mouth quirks. "I look at a lot of beautiful women like that. None of them walk away from me without even a glance. Only you, Alina Madsen."

My full name on his lips makes me shiver. "I guess I'm different."

"Yeah. You definitely are."

He hasn't let go of me yet. He's close enough now that I can feel his breath, warm against my mouth. He traces his thumb along my bottom lip slowly, so slowly, and I realize that I'm not breathing at all anymore.

I part my lips.

His thumb slides in.

I close my eyes and suck and I'm rewarded with a

low grunt. That sound weaves through my body to my nipples, to my pussy. I suck harder, wishing Damian would put a very different body part into my mouth, one that's bigger, longer, thicker, harder.

His free hand sinks into my hair.

I pull back, his thumb sliding free of my lips with a soft pop. I open my eyes to find him watching me, his expression hard with lust. My pulse races, my breath coming in shallow pants.

He leans closer, his lips a breath from mine—

A buzzing sound interrupts, and Damian pulls back from me. I exhale a shuddery breath as he reaches for his phone and puts it to his ear, his gaze still locked on mine.

"What?"

I can hear someone on the other end of the call, but can't make out the words.

"Fine," Damian says. "I'll stop there first."

With that, he stands and pulls me to my feet. He takes my hand and presses it to the hard ridge of his cock, straining against the front of his jeans. Then he presses his mouth to mine in a hard kiss, one that hints at both need and frustration.

"I'll be back later to continue this conversation," he promises.

Or maybe it's more of a warning than a promise.

He grabs the leather jacket draped over the back of one of the chairs and slips the phone into the pocket, already headed for the door before I can even think of a reply.

9

Damian

I LEAVE Vito and Joe to guard Alina while Luca and I head to Dante's penthouse in downtown Vegas.

I'm fucking obsessed. I want to touch every inch of her soft skin, lick her, bite her, make her scream my name. If it was just that—a need to fuck her—I could understand it. But it isn't just that. When she talked about the asshole who killed her parents, I wanted to find him and kill him slowly, bring her his severed head as a gift. I wanted to take her hurt and swallow it, make it my own so it never touches her again. And that makes no fucking sense.

"You want me to come up with you?" Luca asks.

It takes me a second to pull my thoughts from Alina and remember where the fuck I am. "Probably best I go up alone. Leo says Dante's in rough shape. Wants me to slap some sense into him."

Luca nods. "Maybe get him to eat something before you hit him? And careful of that pretty face."

"Mine or his?"

Luca grins. "Definitely not yours."

I take the elevator up and bang on the door, wait a few minutes before banging again. No one answers. I bang again and lean against the door to call, "I know you're here, shithead. Open the fucking door."

I hear a groan, then a thump. Finally, the door opens and the smell of stale booze hits me in a wave.

"You look like shit," I say.

He does. My brother is both handsome and vain. He normally keeps his light brown hair perfectly cut and styled. He's always clean-shaven. He's always dressed smart-casual. He works out on the daily. And his place is usually as impeccable as his grooming.

The man in front of me is dishevelled, his shirt stained, his jaw sporting at least a week's growth of beard. His green eyes are bloodshot, the skin beneath puffy and dark. And he's holding a half-full glass of booze in his hand.

"It's nine o'clock in the morning," I say.

"Never too early to get a head start on the day," Dante says, raises his glass in a toast, then takes a long swallow of his drink.

"When was the last time you ate? Showered? Drank something non-alcoholic?"

"Don't know. Not sure. Don't care," Dante replies, his voice rough and raw.

I push past him and step inside. He closes the door behind me. The place stinks and is wreathed in gloom. The blinds that cover the floor to ceiling windows are closed. There are empty bottles on the coffee table and floor.

I glance up toward the loft. "When was the last time you actually slept in your bed?"

Dante makes a dark, ugly sound. "When was the last time I slept at all?" he asks. "Every time I close my eyes I see blood and brains. Every time I close my eyes, the gun is in *my* hand and I'm the shooter."

Guilt bites me. This is my fault. I told Dante to follow Enzo Bianchi at the casino the night Papa was shot. I gave him that task. And he left Bianchi playing slots to come and meet us for dinner. So he blames himself for Papa's death. He believes that if he had stayed on Bianchi, he could have stopped him.

I grab my brother by the neck and hold him still as I press my forehead to his. "This is not your fucking fault," I say, aware of the irony of my words given that I was just silently blaming myself. "We can all play the 'what if' game. What if I'd sent Cassio to follow him instead of you? What if I'd followed Bianchi myself that night? What if Papa had chosen a different restaurant for dinner? What if, what if, what if. Truth is, there's no going back, only forward. I need you, Dante. Leo needs you. We need you to get your shit together and step up because there are only two things that matter now. The family. And vengeance, cold and sharp. You fucking hear me?"

There's a long pause, the only sound the rasp of my brother's breathing.

"I fucking hear you," Dante whispers.

"Good. Now get in the shower and get dressed. We're meeting Leo in thirty."

My brother heads upstairs and I hear the shower turn on. While he's up there, Luca joins me and together we dispose of the empty bottles, and the full ones. We tidy the place. Open the blinds. Wipe down the coffee table.

I'm no fool. I know this is no solution. My brother can easily replace the bottles I tossed.

But maybe he won't. Maybe.

Luca, Dante, and I arrive at Rosie's Diner, an off-strip greasy spoon that makes killer pancakes. Leo is already seated at a table near the back, away from the windows. There are three other men with him. Two more of his men stand guard outside.

I take a seat across from Leo. Luca sits on one side of me, Dante on the other.

"Where's Cass?" I ask.

"Sent him back to Chicago. He'll be home next week," Leo says.

"Coffee," I say when the waitress comes over. Leo and the others are already tucking into their food.

"What?" Leo asks when I don't add to my order. "Just coffee? You're not hungry?"

"I ate," I say, thinking of the way Alina closed her eyes and savored that first bite of chocolate croissant. There'd been a tiny drop of chocolate at the corner of her mouth. I'd wanted to lean in and lick it away. The tip of her tongue had darted out and done it before I could. Disappointing.

"I didn't eat. Wasn't invited," Luca says, cutting me an amused glance. He orders his meal and Dante orders coffee. Leo studies our brother a moment and amends Dante's order to include a full breakfast—eggs, bacon, toast, pancakes, potatoes, fruit.

"Not sure I can stomach that," Dante says with a wince as the waitress leaves.

"Try," Leo says. He takes a bite of toast, then asks me, "Anything?"

I know he's asking about Bianchi.

"Soon," I say, and he nods. Leo isn't the type to micromanage. He assigns a task and trusts that the person he chose to carry it out will do the job. He knows I'll find Bianchi. And he knows I'll kill him only after I pull everything he knows out of him, along with his blood, bones, organs…whatever it takes to get answers.

"You remember I told you Bianchi was at our casino, following a blonde?" I say, the memory of Alina's long blonde hair wrapped in my fist sliding through my thoughts.

Leo studies me. "Yeah."

"I have her. Tucked in all nice and warm."

Leo sets his knife and fork down carefully, aligning them precisely, his attention appearing to be focused on the task. But I know my brother. His attention is focused solely on me.

"Name?"

I hesitate. For some reason, I don't want to share that information with my brother. Which makes no sense. "Alina Madsen."

"Madsen," he muses. "Any relation to Markus?"

"His sister."

Leo frowns. "Madsen works for us. But his sister was with Bianchi…" He shakes his head. "You don't think something is off about this?"

"That's why I took her. To get information."

"She tell you anything?"

I think of her expression, her voice, the way she looked at me when we spoke of my father's death, of her parents' deaths. I think of the admission she shared, that she'd wanted her parents' killer to suffer, to die. She'd told me a lot of things, but none of them are what Leo wants to know. "Says she doesn't know anything about who Bianchi works for or where he is."

"And you believe her?"

"I do."

Leo looks unconvinced. "You certain she's not an informant? Bianchi brought her onto our turf the night our father died…"

I almost tell him I'm certain. But I don't because I can't be certain. And that pisses me off.

"That's why I'm keeping her at the penthouse, guarded at all times. No one in. No one out. And I took her phone."

Leo nods then pinches the bridge of his nose between his thumb and forefinger. I know the weight of his new position is sitting heavy on his shoulders.

"We should go out on the boat. You, me, Sabina," I say. Dante makes a soft groan. He hates the boat on the best of days, and right now he is not living his best days. "You can stay on shore," I say.

"Appreciated," Dante mutters.

As much as Dante hates the water, Leo loves it.

"Not a bad idea," he says. "A little family time on the water would be good—"

His expression hardens and his gaze shifts to a point beyond my left shoulder. The men on the same side of the table as Leo grow tense, expressions closed and cold. I'm on my feet, turning before I even see the threat, putting myself between my brother and whatever is coming for him, hand reaching for the weapon at my right hip. Beside me, both Dante and Luca rise, the three of us forming a protective wall.

Nikolai Ivanov saunters through the diner, approaching our table, two goons at his back. His dark brown hair is windblown, his blue eyes cold and flat. The lopsided grin he offers doesn't reach his eyes.

"What a coincidence, seeing you gentlemen this morning," Nikolai drawls.

"Not much of a believer in coincidences," I say. "What do you want?"

His lips pull down in an exaggerated frown, "Not happy to see me, Damiano?" He presses his right hand to his chest over his heart. "You wound me to the core."

He turns to Leo.

"Leonardo," he says.

"Nikolai," my brother says.

"My father sent me to remind you that agreements were made between Salvatore and my uncle Vlasta." Nikolai pauses, offering a tight smile. "You assured my father that those agreements will remain intact despite the deaths of your father and my uncle. Yet you overstep, Leonardo. My father will be only so patient before he oversteps in return."

Rage surges. I want to punch the piece of shit in the face, feel the burn in my knuckles, watch his blood drip. Beside me, Luca sidles forward, using his height and bulk to fill the space. Dante rests his hand on his weapon. The goons behind Nikolai tense.

"You've delivered your message," Leo says, his tone mild, a little bored. *You can go now, errand boy*, he doesn't say. He doesn't need to. The implication is clear.

A muscle in Nikolai's jaw ticks, but there's no other evidence of his fury at my brother's dismissal. He stares at Leo, then says, his voice low and hard, "My uncle Vlasta was a fine man. He was good to me. Like a father to me." I notice he doesn't say *second* father. I'm not surprised. Everyone knows Nikolai's father Mikhail is a self-centred bastard. "He was in his prime. Had a full physical a week before he died. There wasn't a damn thing wrong with his heart. Got to wonder if there's anything strange about the fact that he met with your father in the morning and dropped dead of a heart attack in the afternoon."

Leo rises, his gaze never leaving Nikolai's. Where Dante, Cassio, and Sabina look more like our mother, I take after our father. But Leo looks like our grandfather with the same square jaw and razor-sharp cheekbones, the same mouth, his lower lip fuller than his upper. My brother is a handsome man, but in this moment, he looks like a devil, eyes narrowed, burning with fury. With hate. Still, his voice is soft and calm when he says, "Don't look for a snake in my yard, Nikolai, when you have a viper in your own."

Nikolai holds Leo's gaze for a long moment. "Figure your shit out, Leonardo," he says, then he turns and strides out of the diner, his goons behind him.

"Anyone else find it interesting that he said Vlasta was like a father to him even though his actual father is hale and hearty?" Luca asks as we all settle back in our seats.

"Mikhail's a piece of shit. Even to his own kid," Dante says.

"I'm more interested in the fact that Nikolai believes we are responsible for Vlasta's death," Leo says. "Which would give the Ivanovs a motive for the hit on Papa." He looks at me. "We need to find Bianchi." He drums his fingers on the tabletop. "We also need to figure out which agreement Mikhail believes we breached and resolve the issue before it triggers repercussions. Find out, Damian. And deal with it."

10

Alina

I DON'T LIKE FEELING trapped, *being* trapped. But here I am, trapped in a luxurious prison. I'm trapped because the elevator won't move without an access card and because there are two muscle-bound thugs sitting in the foyer, drinking coffee and guarding me. And I'm trapped by my own thoughts and worries.

I keep thinking about Markus, desperate to check on him. But I have no way to reach him because Damian took my phone. I asked the thugs if I could use one of their phones to call my brother. Vito just stared at me. Joe laughed, turning it into a cough when I glared at him. Neither gave me their phone.

I keep thinking about Damian, about the crazy chemistry between us. Stockholm syndrome, much?

With nothing to occupy my thoughts or my hands, I feel like I'm going crazy. I can only watch so many episodes of *Friends* before I start to feel like my brain is starting to decay.

In an effort to release my anxiety, I'm doing jumping jacks in front of the massive white sectional in the living room when the front door opens and Damian enters the condo. He told me he would be back to continue our conversation, and here he is ten hours later. I hate that a part of me is glad to see him.

I'm not claiming to know him very well, or that I'm a mind-reader, but one look from him makes me come to a sudden halt, frozen in place.

He doesn't look friendly. Not that he has in the past, but this is different.

He's wearing dark aviator sunglasses that completely shield his eyes. But there's something in the tightness of his jaw beneath his carefully cultivated three-day stubble that makes my heart double its pace.

"What's wrong?" I ask. "Is it Markus?"

His lips thin. "You're far too concerned about that brother of yours."

"Shouldn't I be?"

"No, you definitely should be. But I'm already sick of hearing about it."

I send him a glare of my own. He takes off his jacket and slings it over a nearby chair. Then he peels off the sunglasses. No man has a right to be this beautiful, especially one who's a monster. Shouldn't monsters look like monsters?

He moves past me and takes a seat on the sofa, as comfortable and relaxed as if he owns the place. Which, I assume he does. He pats the seat next to him. With a glare, I settle as far from him as I can.

"Where's Enzo?" he asks.

"Where's my brother?" I ask.

He offers a dark smile, those perfect lips curving to reveal straight, white teeth. "Markus is fine, last time I checked. He's busily working on making good on his debt." Damian cocks his head. "You probably think I should forgive him for what he owes me, let him walk away, easy as pie, right?"

"No," I reply honestly, tucking my legs underneath me. "He got himself into this situation because he has a gambling addiction. He should pay what he owes and learn his lesson…"

"And yet...?" he prompts when I don't continue.

"And yet," I begin. "A million dollars is a ludicrous amount for a few hands of poker."

"This is Las Vegas. There is plenty of high stakes gambling going on at all hours of the day or night. A million is a drop in the bucket."

"Sharks," I say. "Those are sharks. You're a shark...with sharp teeth and deep pockets. My brother? He's just a little guppy."

He offers a dry laugh. "You think so, do you?"

"I know so." I pause. "Which makes me wonder how he even got a seat at your poker table…"

"I invited him."

"Why?"

He ignores my question, instead asking one of his own. "How long have you been in Vegas, Alina?"

I stumble over the change of subject. "Almost five months."

"So you met Enzo almost as soon as you stepped into the city?"

And we're back to Enzo. "Pretty much."

"How did you meet him?"

"He was at a party."

"Whose party?"

"I don't know. I went with my brother."

Damian leans forward, grabs my ankles and drags me along the couch until I'm right next to him. He could bruise me, hurt me, but his hands are gentle, warm against my skin. He strokes my ankle, my calf. I inhale a shuddering breath and wet my suddenly dry lips.

He traces the tip of his finger along the outside of my thigh to my hip, then cups my chin, his thumb dragging along my lower lip. My pulse is a runaway train, my heart hammering in my chest.

"Beautiful," he murmurs, his eyes lifting to mine. This close, I can see every dark, curled lash.

"I—" I pull free of his touch and look away, unsettled, staring through the floor-to-ceiling windows at the twinkling lights and the Sphere.

"What did you see in Enzo?" he whispers against my ear.

Startled by how close he is, I jerk my attention back to his face. If I move even an inch, my lips will be on his and his on mine. I want to close that distance so badly. Instead, I ease back. Damian Russo isn't just a bad boy. He is a very bad man. A very dangerous man.

And right now, he holds my life and the life of my brother in his hands.

"What did I see in Enzo? The truth is, not much. I didn't know anyone in Vegas except Markus. I was lonely. Bored. Markus took me to a party. When Enzo asked for my number, I gave it to him. When he asked me out, I went. The first couple of times, we had fun. Afterward, he texted me funny memes and jokes. Asked my opinion about things."

"What things?" Damian asks.

"I don't know… music, food, movies, shows…"

"Go on," he says when my voice trails away.

"He seemed so focused on me, so interested. He was charming. Then his façade started to crack. I started to see who he really was. He started dismissing everything I said, telling me my opinions were stupid.

He'd make me change my outfit if he didn't approve of what I was wearing, make me redo my makeup until he was satisfied. He'd order my dinner without asking what I preferred. But every time I tried to pull away, to say no to his invitations, he'd just show up and push his way back into my life. And I was stupid enough to let him."

"Not stupid," Damian says. "Men like him have a way of doing things."

Men like him? What does Damian mean by that? Isn't he just as dangerous as Enzo?

No. He isn't. He's more dangerous, more powerful. And right now, I am completely under his control.

I wrap my arms around myself. "Fuck. I don't want to talk about Enzo," I say, wriggling away from Damian. He lets me go but he watches me with that dark, fathomless gaze.

"But I do," Damian says, his voice a low rumble. "So let's talk."

I shake my head. "I still don't know where he is."

"He's somewhere," he says.

"Or he's dead," I whisper, regretting letting the words out the second they leave my lips.

His jaw tenses. "That would be very inconvenient."

"Why?"

"Because it robs me of the pleasure of killing him myself."

A shiver speeds down my spine.

"I need answers from you, Alina," Damian says.

"I can't tell you what I don't know," I whisper. But I could tell him what I *do* know, what I overheard. Mention of the Ivanovs. Why don't I tell him that? Because it's my one trump card and I'll only play it when I really need it.

"You've been hiding from him, haven't you?" Damian asks.

I shake my head as my heart flutters in my chest.

"You're afraid of him." Damian's voice is a low rumble, luring me to confide in him.

"I said I don't want to talk about Enzo." The words explode out of me.

"And yet, here we are. Talking about that asshole." He strokes a wayward strand of hair off my cheek. "I swear to you, Alina, he will never hurt you again. He will never touch you again."

His words surprise me, as does the intensity of how he's watching me. "Why do you care?"

Damian rears back as if I've slapped him. After a long moment, he says, "Good fucking question. You're nothing to me."

I feel a flush of anger touch my cheeks, and a prick of hurt sting my heart. Which makes absolutely no sense. He's right. I am nothing to him.

"And you're nothing to me," I snap back, forcing a tight smile.

His lips thin. We glare at each other in silence until he asks, "What clubs did he take you to?"

"Clubs?" It takes me a second to catch up with the change of topic. "Um… Hakkasan, Drai's, Voodoo, LED…"

His eyes narrow slightly at the mention of the last one. "What restaurants?"

I huff out a breath. "I don't know. Different places."

"Humor me. Name a few."

"He liked Bottiglia, Settebello, Chen's…"

"Chen's? The hole in the wall in Chinatown?"

I nod. "That's the one. The food there is really good. I mean, really, really good."

He lifts a brow. "Anywhere else?"

"La Vecchia. That was his favorite. He took me there a few times. And each time he'd leave me sitting alone for at least half an hour while he went in back and spoke to the chef."

Damian tenses. "He spoke to the chef at La Vecchia," he muses.

"Does that means something?"

His smile is tight, forbidding, frightening. "Yeah. Actually, it means a great fucking deal."

11

Damian

IT TOOK everything I had to leave Alina last night when what I really wanted to do was get her naked and fuck her. I know dozens of gorgeous women. Sexy, smart, luscious women. But from the second I first saw Alina Madsen, she's the only one I want.

I exhale sharply. What the fuck is wrong with me?

Thinking about Alina brings me back to what she revealed: that piece of shit Enzo Bianchi took her to La Vecchia, a restaurant owned by the Ivanovs.

My phone buzzes. "Markus," I say. "I hadn't expected to hear from you so soon. You have my money already?"

"I have information," Markus says. He sounds nervous, twitchy.

I wait, but he offers nothing more. "And what will this information cost me?" I ask, expecting he'll ask for more time.

He clears his throat. "Information in return and a favor."

"I see. A two for one deal. Why don't you share first so I can determine the value of your information?"

"Narcotics. Heroin, to be precise," he says. "Emanuel Gallo decided he could make some cash on the side. He has a connection with the Mexicans, a guy he grew up with. Decided it would be a good idea to distribute for them. He's been at it for at least three months."

I had every confidence that I would find out the reason Mikhail sent Nikolai to confront my brother at the diner, but I hadn't expected Markus to be the source. Nor had I expected that one of our men would deal narcotics. But neither of those things truly surprise me. Markus is very good at finding out information. He's done several jobs for the family that required that exact skill set. As for the narcotics, greed can make men do stupid things. Especially men like Emanuel Gallo who has strayed from the path twice before.

"Thank you," I say. "And what information would you like in return?"

"My sister. Is she okay?"

"She is more than okay. She is currently living a life of pampered luxury."

"You haven't hurt her?"

Annoyance curls through me. Where was Markus when Enzo was hurting her? My tone is clipped when I reply, "I have not."

He exhales. "Good. Great. Thank you."

Again, silence.

"Why did you let her date Bianchi?" I ask.

"What?" Markus sounds confused.

"Enzo Bianchi. Why did you let your sister date him?"

"Let my sister…?" Markus makes a choked sound. "Have you met Alina? She's perfectly capable of deciding who she wants to date. I don't tell her what to do. As for Bianchi, what the fuck are you talking about? My sister dated that piece of shit?"

And there's my answer. Markus didn't protect Alina because he hadn't even known she was dating Bianchi. The part of me that lives in the modern world understands that Alina has no obligation to clear the men she dates with her brother. The part of me that lives the life I live, does the things I do, is furious that she was left unprotected.

"She met him at a party you took her to."

"I was there looking for the information you asked for about Vlasta's death," Markus says. "Fuck. I had no idea Alina met Bianchi there."

"I want to find him," I say.

Markus knows better than to ask any questions. "I'll ask around," he says.

"And the favor?" I prod.

"Let Alina go. I'll get you everything I owe you. I'll figure it out. Just don't do anything to her. Let her go. She isn't involved in any of this."

Let her go? Just the thought makes a cold rage spread through my veins. Alina is a key to my revenge. For all I know, she hasn't told me everything. She could be hiding information or she might not even realize she knows something of value.

But it's more than that. Letting her go could put her in the way of harm, and that is something I cannot accept. Enzo Bianchi is still out there. He could go after Alina, hurt her, kill her to keep her quiet. The thought of Alina being outside the sphere of my protection curdles my gut.

She isn't going anywhere. She is mine. Mine to care for, to protect. Mine to keep.

Care for? Protect? Where the fuck did those thoughts come from?

She's my fucking prisoner, my collateral.

"Favor denied." I end the call.

"I DOUBLE CHECKED. CHEN'S IS DEFINITELY STILL TRIAD owned. I'm surprised Bianchi went there, but he could have been an emissary," Luca says late that afternoon as we drive through the North Las Vegas mecca of industrial parks and warehouses. My father foresaw the growth of Vegas as a player in the warehousing and distribution industry and invested accordingly. It's one of our legal businesses, along with restaurants, bars, and a couple of car washes. They dovetail nicely with our less than legal businesses, offering ideal means of laundering large sums of cash.

"And both LED and La Vecchia are Ivanov owned," I say. "Which ties Bianchi to Mikhail."

"We know Mikhail ordered the hit on your father," Luca says, his tone laced with suppressed rage.

"Knowing and proving are two different things. If we're going to start a war, we need proof," I say as we pull into a parking lot. There are three other cars here. I recognize all of them.

"Let's hope Alina can provide the proof," Luca says. "You want me to lean on her?"

The thought of anyone leaning on Alina, threatening her, hurting her, makes anger roil inside me. I cut Luca a warning glance. "Whatever information she has will be shared with me and me alone. No one touches her."

Luca grins. "You been hit by the thunderbolt?"

"The what?"

"The Godfather. Michael Corleone. He got hit by the thunderbolt. Love at first sight."

"You watch too many movies." I glower at him. "And who the fuck said anything about love?"

"Actually, I read the book," Luca says with a laugh.

Of course he did.

I exit the car and stride into the warehouse followed by the sound of Luca's laughter. I love the fucker like a brother, but right now I wouldn't mind planting my fist in his face.

The inside of the warehouse is quiet. Late afternoon sunlight filters in through grimy windows set high in the walls, cutting pale lines across the concrete floor. Stacks of crates tower overhead, creating narrow aisles. The place smells of dust and damp and concrete and oil.

Four of our men stand to one side. Frank, a guy around my father's age, detaches from the group and walks toward me.

"Markus' information checks out," he says.

"Shit. So this is what had Nikolai's panties in a wad," Luca mutters.

"Justifiably so," I say, tamping down my fury.

Markus told the truth. One of our men has been dealing heroine. Decades ago, when my father became boss, he put a ban on trafficking narcotics. Any of our people who broke that rule would be killed.

Maybe Papa had scruples. I doubt it. I asked him once, and he said it was because the jail terms for narcotics trafficking were too long. He didn't want to do without valuable men for that length of time if someone got caught. He also said that faced with such a lengthy prison term some men might be tempted to share secrets they had no business sharing in exchange for a lighter sentence.

Two months ago when Leo took over, he made it clear that Papa's rules still apply. Too much risk for too little reward. We don't traffic in narcotics. We leave that lucrative avenue open for others. Like the Ivanovs.

Now, it seems that Emanuel Gallo branched out on his own, getting involved with the Mexicans, not only breaking the rule, and in doing so, making a statement about his disrespect for the family, but also pissing off a rival organization at a time when Leo hasn't yet cemented his power.

"Where is he?" I ask.

"Back room." Frank juts his chin toward the back of the warehouse. "You know this isn't the first time he's stepped out of line."

"I know. But it will be the last," I say. My father dealt with Emanuel twice before, showed him leniency because of his longstanding friendship with Emanuel's dead father. Now both fathers are gone and only the sons are left. Leo has no such friendship with Emanuel.

"You want me to take care of it for you?" Luca asks.

I shake my head. "I'll do it."

Together, we go into the back room where I find Emanuel sitting on a metal chair, hands tied behind his back. He has a black eye and a split lip, telling me he didn't come quietly.

I lean down in front of Emanuel, looking him in the eye. I don't ask for an explanation or an apology. I just wait for him to speak.

"I'm sorry. I'm sorry, Damian," he says, his eyes wild.

"Only because you got caught," I say. He glares at me in silence. "You've been building a little drug empire for yourself for months, haven't you Emanuel?"

I hold his gaze. "The first time you betrayed the

family, skimmed money from collections, my father forgave you—"

"He had three guys beat the shit out of me," Emanuel interrupts.

"He forgave you," I continue as if he hadn't spoken, my voice low and calm. "The second time you got sticky fingers and betrayed the family, my father forgave you again—"

"He cut off my little finger," Emanuel cries, jerking against his bonds.

"This is the third time, Emanuel. There is no forgiveness." I strip off my jacket and hand it to Luca.

I could just kill him, neat and quick, but I need to make an example. My father was boss for decades. He had a reputation and respect. No one accused him of weakness, even when he offered mercy. But Leo hasn't been boss long enough. If he shows even a whisper of anything that could be construed as weakness, the vultures will come to feed.

What I do here will help cement Leo's reputation. It will determine how the loyalty of all those under my brother's command will be maintained.

Emanuel will die here today. But first, he needs to pay in blood for the disrespect and betrayal. I could beat him senseless while he's tied to the chair. But that isn't my way. I'll let him use his fists as I use mine.

At my signal, Frank drags Emanuel to his feet and cuts the rope binding his hands. He's built low and square, a few inches shorter than me and a hell of a lot wider. His legs are thick, as are his arms. And he knows how to use the fists he clenches at his sides.

He shifts foot to foot, sweat beading on his forehead. He doesn't beg for mercy. He knows none will be forthcoming. But from the expression on his face, I think he believes he can still walk away. Take me down and walk away. He is a fool.

He circles me slowly. I turn to watch him as he moves, my eyes on his.

With a hiss, he lunges forward, fists swinging, head down. Brute force. No finesse. I deke right, a rush of air passing my left ear as Emanuel swings and misses. I counter with a swift jab to his midsection. He grunts, cursing as he staggers back.

We circle again.

No one speaks. The only sounds are the rasp of our breathing and the steady hum of a fan somewhere in the distance.

He comes at me again, a right hook. I block, his fist glancing off my forearm. I feel the blow echo through the bone. My uppercut catches his jaw. His head jerks back, a spray of blood and saliva arcing through the air. He shakes his head, dazed for an instant. Then, with a roar, he tackles me. We hit the floor in a tangle of limbs and fists. Adrenaline courses through me, my heart pounding, my focus a red haze as I punch again and again.

When I'm done, Emanuel lies on the ground moaning. My eye is swelling and my cheek burns. I stagger to my feet, breathing hard, blood and sweat streaming into my eyes.

Luca hands me my weapon.

The adrenaline of the fight still pours through me, making my skin feel tight.

Emanuel pushes up on his feet, one hand on the wall for balance. "Please," he begs. "Please."

My gaze meets his and I pull the trigger. One. Twice.

His body jerks. I'm already turning away before he hits the ground.

12

Alina

I'm dozing on the massive couch when a sound wakes me… it might have been the elevator or the front door. The room is dim, only ambient light filtering in from the city beyond the massive windows.

A dark form stalks toward me.

Damian.

Scrambling to a sitting position, I watch as he peels off his jacket. The muscles of his arms stretch the short sleeves of his t-shirt. He tosses the jacket aside then pulls his t-shirt over his head, leaving his torso bare. My breath stops. He's all lean muscle and tattoos—the solid planes of his chest, the ridges of his abdomen, the muscled caps of his shoulders. I've never seen anything so gorgeous. Or so dangerous.

His eyes glitter as he advances toward me, a predator, his muscled frame radiating raw, masculine power.

"Damian?" His name is barely a whisper, a question… an invitation.

"Alina." His voice is a low growl, velvet and whiskey

with a hint of gravel. Just the way he says my name sends a shiver of lust through me.

I surge to my feet as he comes nearer, then back away.

"This is a bad idea," I whisper.

"A terrible idea," he agrees. "And I don't fucking care."

There's something wild about him tonight. Something feral and dark.

Well…darker than usual.

"Did something happen?" I ask, clicking on the lamp. I gasp. His hair is a damp, tousled mess. His right eye is swollen and bruised, his knuckles cracked and bloody. And he's staring at me with brazen hunger, like he wants to eat me alive.

"Something happened," he says. "And I came here. To you. Don't fucking ask me why because I have no fucking clue."

"I—"

"Take your clothes off, Alina." A command. It touches something deep inside me, something that aches to obey. His words, the low tone of his voice, the expression on his face all turn me on.

Still, I shake my head, backing away until there's nowhere for me to go, my back pressed against the cool glass of the window.

"Please," I whisper, but I don't know what I'm asking for.

He keeps coming until he's a foot away, his gaze roaming my face, my body. "Clothes. Off."

I stare at him, my heart pounding, my mouth dry. I could tell him to go. I could say no.

But I don't.

The seductress buried deep inside me roars to life,

wanting—needing—his eyes on me. Slowly, so slowly, I peel off my top. I'm not wearing a bra. My nipples harden in the cool air. His gaze drops to my naked breasts, his expression hungry and savage, twisting a knot of desire low in my belly. I hook my thumbs in the waistband of my yoga pants and panties, shimmy them down over my hips, my thighs, my calves, then I kick free of them and straighten, my chin high, shoulders back.

In one swift motion, he pulls me to him. His lips are on mine, demanding and fierce. Teasing. Tormenting. Tongues tangling, teeth grazing, a clash of dominance and submission.

He kisses me like I am air to a drowning man, like I am all he needs or will ever need.

Heat roars along my veins, leaving me dizzy and weak. He has one arm around my waist. If it wasn't, I'd be a boneless puddle on the floor. His free hand roams up my body, leaving a trail of fire in its wake. Tangling his fingers in my hair, he tips my head back. His lips move to my neck, sucking, biting, leaving marks. Want and need arrow through me. He smells incredible, hints of citrus and musk.

I twine my fingers in his damp hair, silky soft.

He tastes me, his tongue moving down my neck, over my collarbone, then tracing the swell of my breast. He takes my aching nipple in his mouth, licks the sensitive peak, bites me, just hard enough to make me cry out and arch my back. He pinches my other nipple, his fingers wicked, making me whimper. Panting, I pull him closer, aching for his touch.

Rearing back, he studies me, his eyes dark and fathomless, heavy lidded with lust.

"Hands above your head," he orders.

The words coupled with the tone of his voice reach

inside me and make me long to obey his every command. My back presses to cool glass as I lift my arms and press the backs of my hands against the window.

His mouth moves hungrily on mine, exploring, tasting. Claiming. His kiss is like the best wine, like ambrosia. Hot, heavy, raunchy lust spirals through me. My heart races, my legs tremble.

His hand slides to my hip, then lower, his fingers easing between my legs. "So wet for me," he murmurs, his voice low and rough. "So tight."

I moan as he slides his fingers inside me, curling them to touch me exactly the way I need. I reach for him and he stills, denying me.

"Hands above your head, Alina. Keep them there. You move only when I give you permission."

"Damian." His name is a plea, a prayer. I want to touch him. I want to feel the hard planes of his body. I want to wrap my fist around his cock.

My legs wobble. I feel swollen, aching, on fire… my breasts, my pussy. I've never been this turned on in my life.

He lifts me and carries me to the couch, setting me down on my back, arranging my body the way he wants. Hands above my head. Knees bent. Legs splayed, leaving me fully open to him.

Suddenly shy, I start to bring my knees together, but with a dark laugh he pushes them apart, even wider than they were before. And I let him. His lips curl in a dark smile as he stares down at me.

"Good girl," he murmurs, then leans down and kisses me, hot and wild. I arch into his kiss, but keep my limbs exactly as he placed them. I'm naked. He's still wearing his jeans, a power imbalance that turns me on.

He kisses his way down my body, sucking first on one

nipple, then the other. Kissing the edges of my ribs. Tracing his tongue around my belly button. Lower. He runs his tongue along my center in a slow glide. Again he licks me, and again. I arch and whimper as his tongue swirls around my clit, then his lips suck and pull. He teases me, his tongue working in slow circles as he palms my breasts, playing with my nipples while he licks my clit. Pinching. Twisting.

A moan escapes me and my hips shift restlessly forward and back. "I need… please… I need…"

He makes a low laugh. "Patience, Alina."

There's only Damian. The feel of his hands on my breasts, his mouth on my clit.

He uses his teeth, just hard enough to make me cry out. He uses his tongue, slow and gentle, then faster, working me to a frenzy.

I gasp. I sigh his name. I moan.

Please. Please. Yes, like that. Just like that. So close. So close…

He torments me until I am writhing and begging, my need so exquisite I feel like I'm going to combust. Then he presses his tongue firmly against my clit as he pushes his fingers inside me and I come so hard I scream, my back bowing off the couch, my heart slamming against my ribs. He eases the pressure of his tongue, gentle now, letting me ride the waves of my orgasm, drawing them out in an endless ribbon.

I don't know how long I lie there, unable to move, his big hands stroking my arms, my legs, my belly, gentle, soothing.

Rising to his feet beside the sectional, he stares down at me, eyes glittering in the lamplight, lips curved in a feral smile. His gaze holds mine as he undoes his jeans. His cock springs free, long and thick and hard.

I lick my lips.

"What do you want?" he asks.

Choices, choices. I want his cock in my mouth. I want it in my pussy.

"I want you to fuck me," I say. And I do. Oh, god. I've never wanted anything more than I want Damian's cock inside me, stretching me, filling me. I cut him a sidelong look through my lashes. "Please."

He laughs, low and rough. "Since you ask so nicely…"

I watch while he slides on a condom. He flips me face down before pushing a cushion under my belly and positioning my legs, knees bent. He kneads my ass. "Fuck. You have a gorgeous ass."

He lands a light slap on my right cheek, then a harder one on my left. I squirm but don't protest. Why don't I protest? Because I like it. I like the feel of his palm on my ass, the sting, the promise of what will come after.

He reaches down and strokes my pussy, then pulls the moisture up between my cheeks, letting the tip of his finger graze my asshole. I make a mewling sound and try to pull away but he presses his palm against the small of my back, holding me still. "Not today, pretty girl. Today I'm going to fuck your gorgeous pussy. But it's only a matter of time before I make every inch of you mine."

Shifting closer, he positions himself at the opening of my pussy, pushing the wide head of his cock into me, just a little, just enough to make me want more. I arch and squirm, but he takes his time, squeezing my ass cheek while he stretches me. God, he's so big, so hard. He pulls back just a little, pushes forward a little more, the glide slow and slick and I ache to set a rhythm, a pattern.

"You're so fucking wet," he says. "So tight."

With a moan, I arch, needing him to fill me. "Please," I whisper.

"Such a good, greedy girl," he says, and shoves his cock all the way in.

He fills me, his cock deep inside me, his hand kneading my ass.

Taking his time, he pumps in, out, a slow tease, making me writhe and rock and ache, feeding the lust roaring through me. Each thrust pulls me deeper into mindless need. There's only Damian, the feel of him, the scent of him.

"Please," I whisper. "Please. Please."

His fingers find my clit and he strokes me as his thrusts grow faster, rougher, deeper.

I'm so close. So close. So—

He thrusts hard and holds still and I feel him throbbing inside me as he comes, my own orgasm crashing through me. I scream my release, my world spinning, heart hammering. I collapse beneath him, his chest against my back, the weight of him pinning me.

I lie there slowly coming back to myself. My only thought is that I just had the best sex of my entire life. Whatever happened to Damian tonight, he brought his pain and need and rage and desire to me. He came to *me.*

And that I am secretly, darkly glad that he did.

I am so screwed.

13

Damian

ALINA LIES next to me in the big bed, her legs intertwined with mine, my arm around her, her head on my shoulder. She is the fucking hottest thing I've ever known.

"So...what was that all about?" she asks.

"Is that a complaint?" I say, tipping my head so I can look down at her.

"Definitely not." Her lush lips curve in a smile that makes me want to kiss her. "It's just...if you want to talk, I'm a good listener."

I'm quiet for a moment, surprised to find that I do want to talk. It's an uncharacteristic inclination, one I can't give in to. Telling Alina about what happened at the warehouse is not in the cards.

Still, I find myself saying, "There are things about my job that I do not enjoy." That's an understatement.

I'd left Luca to supervise the clean-up at the warehouse. Get rid of the body. Hose everything down. I'd called Leo to let him know Nikolai's concern had been dealt with. I'll fill him in in person. Some things we don't discuss on the phone. Definitely don't put in a text.

I'd headed to my place, showered, changed my clothes. But I'd been wired, the kind of wired that needs release before it incinerates everything it touches.

I'd intended to drive out to the desert and let the night sky and open road burn off the sensation of my skin being too tight. Instead, I'd found myself at the penthouse.

Just seeing Alina had quieted the burn in my veins a little.

Fucking her had quieted it a lot.

I've wanted her since the first moment I saw her. That wanting was nearing obsession. I'd thought that having her would change that. It didn't. Now that I've tasted the forbidden fruit, I just want her more. I want every part of her. Every morsel.

She sits up and looks down at me, dragging the sheet to her chest. "There are things about your job that you don't enjoy? Seriously?"

She sounds…incredulous? No. There's a bite of sarcasm in her tone.

"Seriously," I say, wary.

A small laugh escapes her. "You're very spoiled."

"What?" I'm as much startled by her words as by the fact that she had the brass balls to say them.

"You had to do something for work that you didn't enjoy and that sent you here stalking me like a predator?"

It's my turn to laugh. "I wouldn't exactly put it like that."

"How would you put it?"

"I didn't stalk you. I fucked you."

She offers a satisfied smirk. "Yes, you did. Very efficiently."

"Efficiently? Meaning, what?"

"You fucked me well."

"Well?" I take her hand and nip at the tip of her index finger.

"Passionately."

"Better," I say, and nip the tip of her middle finger.

"Erotically," she says, laughter lacing the word.

I nip her ring finger.

"Sensually."

I nip her little finger. "More."

"Mind-blowingly."

"I'll accept that," I say, surprised by the ease between us. I am not the type to linger after sex. The fact that I want to be here, in this bed with Alina, is unusual for me.

She leans down and presses her mouth to mine in a soft kiss. Then she gently touches my cheek. "You need ice for that cheek and that eye."

Before I can stop her, she bounds out of bed, taking the sheet with her and dragging it around her naked body. I'm disappointed that she's blocking my view. She heads to the kitchen and I hear her puttering in there before she returns with some ice wrapped in a dishcloth. Climbing back onto the bed beside me, she sits cross-legged and lowers the ice to my face.

Her expression is focused, intent, her hands gentle. An odd feeling suffuses me. When was the last time someone took care of me like this? I honestly can't fucking remember.

"So what is it about your job that you don't enjoy?" She repositions the ice so it's more comfortable for me. Not sure how she knows what would be more comfortable, but somehow, she does. "Does it have something to do with that brand-new shiner you have?"

"There are elements of my job that are necessary but unpleasant. Today included those elements." I pause and decide to be honest. "I didn't actually plan to come here tonight. I went home. Showered. Figured I'd settle in for the night. Next thing I know, my keys are in the ignition and I'm driving. Didn't even know where I was heading until I pulled into the underground. And if you ask me to explain why I came, I don't think I'll be able to give you an answer."

She smirks. "You wanted to fuck me."

"Yeah."

I did. I do. But it's more than that. I just wanted to be with her and that makes no fucking sense.

She's quiet for a moment, studying my face. "Everyone has parts of their job that they dislike. Some people hate everything about their job, but they don't have a lot of choices. Do you think I like slinging drinks to a bunch of drunk assholes while wearing a polyester micromini and a halter with no bra? Those are elements of my job that are shitty but necessary. If I want to earn good tips, I do what the job demands. The only times I like my job are when I count my tips or cash my paycheck."

"Then why do that job? Why not just do something else?"

"Are you serious right now?" When I don't reply, she takes my silence for an answer and says, "I'm twenty-three years old with no degree and little job experience. Sure, I could waitress at a restaurant or work as a cashier but I'd make shit money for just as many hours. I don't have a resume that will get me an office job. And I don't have the knowledge that will get me hired as a dealer at one of the casinos. So I work the job that earns me the best paycheck. The only thing I am qualified for that would make me better money is shimmying around a pole naked, and I'm just not comfortable doing that."

It's my turn to study her in silence, digesting her words. The thought of her returning to the Emerald as a waitress, or any place like it, makes me want to punch something. The idea of her dancing naked is even worse. "If you had a choice, what would you do?"

She pushes her hair out of her face, tucking the long strands behind her ear. "Finish my degree."

"English lit, right?"

She nods, then shrugs. "Not that a degree in English lit is a springboard to a high paying job. But communication skills are important. And you said if I had a *choice.* In a perfect world, my choice would be to finish my degree with a concentration in creative writing." She looks away, a pretty blush staining her cheeks. "I, um…I like to write."

"What have you written?" I ask.

"Some short stories. And I've started a couple of novels, but never really made any headway."

"Have you had anything published?"

"One of the short stories. In an online magazine." She glances at me through her lashes. "They paid me. Five hundred dollars. I know that doesn't sound like a lot to you, but it's a lot for a short story." She clears her throat and readjusts the ice again. "What about you? If you had a choice, what would you do?"

"Me?" I think for a second and then answer honestly. "In a perfect world, I'd be exactly who I am, doing exactly what I do."

"Even though there are parts of your job that you don't like."

"Even though," I say. "My job isn't just a job. It's my family, my calling, my destiny, my identity. It's part of who I am, for better or worse."

I study her face, making sure she understands what I am telling her.

Family first. Always.

14

Alina

I WAKE ON MY SIDE, Damian's long body pressed against my back, his arm draped over me.

I had the best sex of my life with a man who is holding me prisoner.

Worse, I *like* the man who is holding me prisoner. I like that he listens when I speak, that he considers my words and questions. I like that he chose to share a little of himself with me. I like that he didn't lose his temper when I called him spoiled.

I like the man who holds my brother's life in his hands. Who holds my life in his hands.

A man who is a criminal, a killer, a villain.

A man who is holding me as collateral on a debt.

I have no illusions about who and what he is.

And yet…I like him.

I wriggle out from under Damian's arm and rise, goosebumps prickling along my arms in the cool air. I grab my robe and shrug it on, wondering what time it is. Leaning over, I check his phone where it sits on the night table. It's late. Or early. Depending on one's perspective.

Wait. Damian's phone.

Adrenaline kicks my pulse up a notch.

I glance at him.

This is my chance to call Markus, to make sure he's okay. I hesitate. Maybe I should just wake Damian and ask. But what if he says no? He'll probably say no.

But I've been so worried…

I kneel down beside the bed and slowly, so slowly, slide the phone across the sheets toward Damian's hand. He doesn't move, doesn't stir, just keeps on breathing, slow and deep and even. I use his thumb to unlock the phone. It takes me three tries, three long, endless tries, my heart in my throat the whole time.

And then it's unlocked and I bound from the room. I close the bedroom door behind me and quickly cross to the second bedroom at the opposite end of the condo.

After closing that door behind me, I start to dial Markus' number, a little surprised when he comes up as a contact. But I guess that makes sense. Damian would want to have his number to follow up on the repayment schedule.

My call goes straight to voicemail.

I hesitate for a second and then say, "Markus, it's me. Just want to let you know that I'm okay. Everything is okay. Damian is treating me well. Don't worry about me. Take care of yourself. I—" I almost tell him I love him. But that will definitely make him worry. Instead, I say, "I'll see you soon," and end the call.

I stand there in the dark, my thoughts spinning. I wish Markus had answered. I wish I could have spoken to him. I have no idea if he has a plan, if he's been able to find his ex-girlfriend and the missing money, if he's managed to gather any funds at all.

But maybe he's texted Damian. Maybe…

Curious, I check the text history.

I'm surprised to see that it goes back months… no, years. I thought Markus just met Damian the night of the poker game. But no, that can't be right. Because before Markus made that idiotic double-or-nothing bet that brought his total to a million fucking dollars, he said that he owed Damian a hundred grand from *that night* but he owed him a total of five hundred grand. Which meant that wasn't the first time they'd played.

I scroll through the texts. There's nothing specific. No chit chat. No friendly ribbing. I read everything carefully and realize that it's just a series of texts where Damian summons Markus and Markus confirms, or Markus texts a single word: *done*. A couple of times he texts: *usual place*. There are no addresses or times or details. My gut is telling me that not all these texts are about poker games. Maybe none of them are. Markus has been doing something for Damian for at least two years, some sort of job. My stomach drops.

Neither Markus nor Damian lied to me about their relationship, but they haven't told me the whole truth, either. I get that Damian owes me no explanations, but why didn't my brother tell me he was working for the Russos? And if Markus was working for the Russos, why was he at the party where I met Enzo, who I'm pretty sure works for the Ivanovs?

Was Markus spying for Damian?

A faint noise makes me jump.

On silent feet, I walk to the living room. The glow of the city lights outlines the silhouettes of the island, the table, the sectional. The door to the other bedroom is still closed.

I need to get Damian's phone back to the night stand before he realizes it's gone.

I look down at the screen as a text comes through. It's from Luca. Two words: *tutto finito.*

I don't speak Italian, but I'm guessing that means *finished* or *done.*

I wonder if whatever Luca is texting about has anything to do with Damian's mood when he arrived.

A hand grabs my wrist.

I scream and jerk away on instinct, landing a solid kick to my attacker's shin.

No. Not an attacker. Damian. His features are cast in light and shadow, accenting the hard line of his jaw, the bruise under his eye. He looks brutal, menacing, the demon-angel I thought him to be the first time I saw him.

"Find what you were looking for?" he asks, his tone cold as arctic ice.

He reaches for me.

I flinch away. Is this the moment he hits me?

The second the thought forms, I push it away. I don't pretend that Damian isn't a monster of some sort, but whatever type of monster he is, my gut tells me he won't hurt me that way.

He freezes. He saw me flinch. I read it in his expression. But he makes no comment. He only says, "Answer me, Alina. Did you find what you were looking for?"

"Yes. No. I wasn't—"

He pulls the phone from my grasp.

"I wasn't looking for anything. I was trying to call Markus. I just wanted to talk to him, to make sure he's okay. I left him a message telling him I'm fine and he shouldn't worry."

Damian checks the call log.

"I'm telling the truth," I say, wondering why I feel hurt that he doesn't believe me.

"Who else did you call?" he asks. His tone would make icicles shiver.

"No one. You just checked the call log. You can see—"

"Easy enough for you to erase," he says.

"I didn't erase anything."

"You accessed my phone without permission," he says.

"I…" I swallow. "I just wanted to talk to my brother."

"Then why didn't you ask?" His eyes bore into mine.

"Because you would have said no."

He nods. "So you went behind my back, took my phone, accessed it without my permission and scrolled through my call log, my texts…What exactly were you looking for, Alina?"

I'm about to say that I didn't look at his texts or call log, that I only tried to call Markus, but that would be a lie. I did look.

"I wasn't looking for anything. It isn't like that. But… does my brother…does he work for you…?" My voice trails away as I look into his eyes. They're dark and flat and emotionless.

Gone is the man who kissed me, touched me, made me scream his name. Who shared his thoughts with me and let me see a little of who he really is. Now Damian is a cold stranger, his expression unreadable.

He turns from me and walks into the bedroom. I stand there, my arms wrapped around myself, uncertain why I feel like I let him down. That is some warped and twisted shit. He's the one holding me prisoner, denying me access to the rest of the world, denying me access to my brother.

He comes back out of the bedroom, fully dressed.

"You're pissed off because I tried to call my brother?" I'm angry now. Furious. "What would you do if someone was holding you prisoner, holding you as collateral for a debt? Because that's what I am. I'm your prisoner." I fan my arm in front of me. "This is my prison. I can't leave. I can't call anyone. I'm just here for you to come by and fuck. If the tables were turned, would you just take that lying down? Or would you grab an opportunity if it presented itself?" My anger fizzles, leaving sadness in its wake. "I just wanted to check on my brother," I finish, my voice soft.

"What were you looking for, Alina? Information? Contacts?" he asks, as if he didn't hear a word I fucking said. "Who do you work for?"

"Work for—?" I shake my head. "I wasn't looking for anything. I was trying to call my brother."

"There is nothing on my phone for you to find, but had you found something, were you going to pass it on to Enzo?"

"Enzo? I don't know where he is. I have no way to reach him. And even if I did, he would be the very last person on earth I would contact."

He quirks one dark brow. "And I should believe you, why?"

"Because it's the fucking truth!" I yell.

But I'm yelling at his back because he's already opening the front door, leaving. He closes it softly behind him. I think it would have been easier if he'd slammed it, if I'd warranted his anger. But apparently Damian Russo doesn't think I'm worth even that.

And why the hell does that hurt so much?

15

Alina

I WAKE up angry and hurt. To keep myself busy, I clean the condo from top to bottom, wash all the towels and linens, and run the dishwasher. I even wash the outdoor furniture on the balconies. Luca keeps telling me it isn't my responsibility, but I need to do *something*. Finally, he just shrugs, goes back to reading and lets me have at it.

The next day, I'm still angry and hurt. But I want to talk to Damian, to sit down like two adults. I guess he isn't on the same page because I don't hear from him, let alone see him. Bored and restless, I open the front door. Vito sits on a folding chair in the foyer between the door and the elevator.

He gets up and asks, "Do you want me to take you somewhere?" He actually looks hopeful. He has to be even more bored than I am.

"No, thanks. Just checking. You, um, want some coffee?"

"Sure. Black, thanks," he says.

So I get him his coffee and close the door. A few

minutes later, someone knocks. I open the door to find Joe.

"You got any more coffee?" he asks.

"Sure. How do you like it?"

"Black, thanks," he says.

So I get him his coffee and close the door.

A few minutes later, there's a knock. I open the door to find both Vito and Joe standing there.

"You, uh, wanna play poker?" Vito asks, looking hopeful.

"I don't have any money," I say. "To bet," I clarify when they both just stare at me.

"You got any cookies? Crackers?" Joe asks.

"Crackers? Um, I think so." I fetch the box of cheese crackers I discovered the first night I was here.

"Okay," Vito says. "We'll play for crackers."

We do. I lose, a lot. Then I finally win a hand, recouping some of my lost crackers.

"I'm done," I say. They both look at me, confused.

"Done?" Joe asks.

"Done," I say. "Done playing."

"But you're winning," Vito says.

"And that's why I'm done," I say. "I'm quitting while I'm ahead."

They both look at me like I'm a strange curiosity.

I change into workout clothes and they follow along without complaint when I head down to the condo gym. They stick to me like glue, glowering at a guy who wanders in. He quickly wanders back out again. I run on the treadmill. I use the free weights. Then I head to the pool and do laps until my arms feel like overcooked spaghetti.

"You can swim," Joe says, sounding surprised.

"I can," I agree, not sure why he made the observation. "Can you?"

"Yeah. I mean, I can make my way across the pool. But you swim like they do in the Olympics. You do that whole roll at the end thing."

I laugh. "Definitely not like they do in the Olympics. But I was on the swim team in high school."

"Nice," Joe says.

"Can we go back inside?" Vito asks. "It's hot as controlled nuclear fusion out here."

"The fuck?" Joe says.

"What?" Vito shrugs. "I saw a show."

"Why don't you guys watch me from right in there?" I suggest, indicating the doors five feet away.

They hesitate for a second, then step inside the doors to the air-conditioned interior while I sit by the pool in the shade—it's too hot for sun.

It's a bit cooler in the evening, so I go for a long walk, my poker buddies stalking along in my shadow.

The next day, Vito and Joe are nowhere to be found. Instead, Luca shows up with three paperbacks: a romance novel, a thriller, and an epic fantasy. I devour the romance novel. Unfortunately, it's a spicy read, which only makes me think of Damian.

In the evening, Luca insists we go for a drive. He takes me to an ice cream place and buys me a pint of Campfire S'mores and a pint of Sea Salt Caramel. He gets himself a pint of Grazacado.

"Seriously? Who wants to eat avocado and olive oil ice cream?" I ask, incensed.

We're sitting on the balcony looking out at the lights. He holds out the laden spoon toward me. "Don't knock it till you try it."

"No, thank you," I say, taking a spoon of my own ice cream.

I'm not ashamed to admit that I eat the entire pint. Sue me. It's my dinner.

Maybe it's because of ice cream overdose, or maybe I miss Damian, but I sleep poorly that night and wake up feeling morose. Three days without a word from him. I almost decide to crawl back under the covers and spend the day feeling sorry for myself, but that just isn't me. So I get up, shower, dress, and head to the kitchen to make coffee.

The kitchen island boasts a box and a bag.

Just then, I hear the front door open behind me. My heart gives a hard thump and I can't help the smile that curves my lips. It dims when I turn to see Luca.

"There's coffee if you want some," I say, feeling awkward. He has to have seen the expectation and joy on my face. And he has to have seen the disappointment. I feel a hot flush stain my cheeks and look down so my hair falls forward. The curse of pale skin. My blush gives my thoughts away.

Problem is, I can't untangle the hot mess of my emotions. I should hate Damian. But I don't. I should hate the men he's left to guard me. But I don't. I should hate everything about my current situation. But I don't.

I definitely need a therapist.

Luca fixes himself a coffee—one sugar, no cream—and settles at the kitchen island on the farthest stool. "You gonna open that?" He gestures at the box.

"Is it for me?" I ask.

He shrugs. "It isn't for me."

I open the box. It's an AlphaSmart Neo 2.

"What's this?" I ask.

"Looks like it's an AlphaSmart Neo 2," Luca says.

I shoot him a look and find his hazel eyes watching me with amusement.

Luca pulls out his phone, types something, looks at me and says, "It's a portable word processor." He looks at his phone for another minute. "Not sure where Damian found this thing. Says here that they don't make them anymore but writers snap them up second hand."

Writers snap them up.

"But don't worry, it doesn't have internet access," he says with that smug look that I've never seen anyone pull off quite as well as he does. "Apparently, no internet access means no distractions. At least, that's what the reviews say."

No internet because Damian doesn't want me to have access to the outside world. Not unless I'm chaperoned and supervised.

"What's in the bag?" Luca asks.

I pull out a half dozen lined pads and a bunch of pens in different colors. And two books: *Techniques of the Selling Writer* by Dwight V. Swain and *Writing Fiction for Dummies*. I decide not to take that as an insult.

"Damian dropped all of that off early this morning," Luca says.

My head jerks up and my pulse kicks up a notch. "Damian was here?"

Luca nods.

He was here early this morning and he didn't wake me. He was here and he didn't stay long enough to see me. He was here and he left me all of these wonderful things.

I'm quiet for a moment, digesting the fact that even angry with me, Damian has just bought me the best gift I've ever received.

I told him I like to write, so he bought me a word processor. And pens and pads and books.

Is it a gesture of apology or forgiveness? I have no way to know unless he actually shows up here to talk to me.

And what is wrong with me that I want him to?

Luca's phone buzzes. He answers and his gaze flicks to mine, then he wordlessly holds the phone out to me. I take it from his hand and bring it to my ear.

"Hello?" I say, my pulse kicking up a notch.

"I'll be there at eight tonight," Damian says, his voice a little rough. "I want to fuck you. If your answer is yes, be naked and waiting in your bed. If your answer is no, don't be there. Have Luca take you out for a walk."

He hangs up before I can say anything.

But we both already know what my answer will be.

16

Damian

ALINA MADSEN PISSES me the fuck off. Because she won't get out of my thoughts. Because I'm furious that she took my phone, that I was careless enough to leave it where she could get it. And I'm even more furious that I see her point. She's my prisoner, collateral for her brother's debt, no contact with him or anyone in the outside world. It isn't hard to believe that she'll do anything to make sure he's okay.

But what if that's all an act, a lie? What if she *was* searching my phone for information?

I can't make myself believe that, and that's part of the problem. Where Alina is concerned, my thoughts aren't rational or orderly. They're primitive, possessive, protective. And that's dangerous.

I park in front of the house in Summerlin, taking a moment before I head inside to meet with Leo. He moved back into the family home right after Papa was murdered. It was either move our sister Sabina into his condo with him or move here and let Sabina stay put. Truth is, the condo would have been hell to secure. The place in Summerlin is a fortress, a contemporary house set on almost four acres with metal gates, an electrified fence surrounding the entire compound, and guards patrolling the perimeter.

To the west, sunset turns the clouds pink against the backdrop of the mountains. I walk toward the front door, the path comprised of massive concrete rectangles that appear to float on a bed of water and river rock. I'm outside but might as well be inside because the house is designed to surround the courtyard. I open the door and step inside.

Leo waits in the entryway. He wraps me in a hug. He's wearing workout gear, and when he steps back, I see that he looks tired.

"You okay?" I ask, knowing that he isn't. All his life, he was trained to take over when the time came, but we thought that time would be when Papa retired many years from now, maybe even decades.

"All good," Leo says, and I don't call him on the obvious untruth.

Cassio ambles over from the kitchen. He looks the most like our mother, blue eyes, thick, wavy blond hair, a straight, slightly broad nose. His lips have a natural upturn at the corners that make him look like he's always smiling. And most of the time, he is.

"Cass," I say, thumping his back with a one-armed hug. "You look good."

"Damian," he says, returning the hug. "You look broody as fuck. Nice shiner. I'm a little put out that you didn't invite me to join the party."

"Anyone seen Dante today?" I ask, glancing between my brothers.

"Had dinner with him last night," Cassio says.

"Did that include food or just drink?" Leo asks.

"Steaks. Baked potatoes. Salad. And a lot of wine," Cassio says.

"At least he's eating," I say.

We follow Leo to his office at the back of the house. Floor to ceiling windows offer a view of the pool and hot tub and, in the distance, the mountains. The tennis court is at the back of the property on the other side of the pool house which is Sabina's territory, a two thousand square foot, two-bedroom, two-bathroom home where she can have both privacy and safety.

"You hungry?" Leo asks me.

"No, but I'll take a beer."

He fetches three from the beverage fridge on the far wall. We settle in three of the four overstuffed brown leather chairs.

"Tell me," he says.

So I do. I tell him about Emanuel. I tell him about Markus supplying the information about Emanuel and the fact that I asked him to look into Bianchi.

"Good call," Leo says.

"Markus has a knack," Cass says.

Leo tells us about the conversation he had with Mikhail and the reassurance Leo offered that the unfortunate overstep will not happen again.

"I had to stand there and smile and shake his hand when what I really wanted to do was push the point of my knife through his heart," Leo says. "He set up the hit on Papa. We all know it." He clenches his jaw. "But instead I had to make nice and send him a case of that Bordeaux he likes."

"It's what Papa would have done," I say. Leo offers a small smile, accepting that as the compliment it's intended to be.

"Only go to war if there is no other choice," Cass

says, quoting our father.

"Oh, we'll be going to war," Leo says. "The second I have proof that bastard set up the hit, we'll be going to war." He looks at me. "Any progress on proving that Vlasta's death wasn't natural?"

"I'm working on the coroner," I say. "Autopsy lists cause of death as rupture of myocardium due to acute myocardial infarction."

When my brothers stare at me blankly, I say, "Heart attack."

They nod.

"But I want to see the tox report. Something caused that heart attack and my gut is telling me poison," I say.

"Poison is a snake's weapon," Leo says. "And Mikhail is a snake."

"Can't argue that," Cass says.

Leo's expression turns thoughtful as he studies me. "Something isn't sitting right with you, Damian. Is it Emanuel? You made a good choice there. I would have done the same."

"I know."

He nods. "So if not that, then what?"

I tell him about Alina and the phone.

"Fuck," Cassio says on a slow exhale.

"You get rid of it?" Leo asks.

"Of course. Destroyed it immediately and got a replacement." Just in case she'd somehow managed to install spyware.

"She's a spy," Leo says.

I don't want her to be, but what I want might have no bearing on reality. Was she telling me the truth? Was she just trying to get in touch with Markus?

"She's working for the Ivanovs," Leo says.

I would be a fool not to consider it. The possibility

grinds at me. Devastates me. If she's a fucking spy, a threat to my family…

"I'll have someone collect her and question her," Leo says.

"You will not." I barely manage to keep the words civil. "No one touches her. No one hurts her." The thought of anyone but me touching that pale skin ignites a rage I've never felt before.

Leo's brows lift.

"You fuck her?" Cassio asks.

"None of your fucking business."

Leo laughs, his smile reaching his eyes, the tension and weight of his position melting away for a minute. "You fucked her." He pauses. "That doesn't change my opinion. She's a spy."

"And your opinion doesn't change mine. I don't think she is. Markus has proven his loyalty time and again."

"Markus has," Leo says, "His sister hasn't."

"Besides, Markus is an addict," Cass points out. "An addict's loyalty isn't reliable."

I have no argument for that. "Alina isn't an addict."

"But she's a spy," Leo says.

We sit in silence for a few moments, drinking our beers.

Then Leo says, "Bring her on the boat. I'd like to have a conversation with her."

And much as I'd like to tell him to fuck off, it isn't a request. It's an order, one that he gave not as my brother but as the head of my family.

An order I will obey because that is who we are, how we live. How we survive.

Problem is, if Leo decides Alina is a threat, he'll kill her. And he'll expect me to go along with it.

Family first. Always.

17

Alina

It's 8:00.

I sit on the white sectional, my hair loose around my shoulders, hanging down my back. No makeup. I'm wearing a pair of ripped jeans and a ratty, oversized sweatshirt with sleeves that fall all the way to my fingertips. There is absolutely nothing sexy about me at this moment, but from the look on Damian's face, he doesn't agree.

"You are not naked in the bed," he says as he stalks toward me, his tone making it clear that he is not pleased. He's wearing a suit tonight, single breasted, the bottom button of the jacket undone. White shirt. Dark tie. Just thinking about sliding his jacket off his broad shoulders, undoing his white shirt, pulling it from the waistband of his pants…

I exhale slowly, watching him warily as he pours himself a whiskey from the well-stocked bar and takes a sip, studying me over the rim of the glass.

"I am also not out for a walk with Luca," I point out.

"Clearly. So instead of choosing one of the options I

gave you, you created one of your own." He takes another swallow of his drink. "The answer was either yes or no, Alina. I didn't give you the option to choose maybe."

"We need to talk," I say.

His gaze flicks over me. "Barefaced and dressed in near-rags, you still make my cock hard," he says, his voice a rough rasp. The way he looks at me just confirms his words.

I shake my head. "We need to talk."

"We need to fuck," he says, setting his unfinished drink aside.

"Not until wc talk."

"There is nothing to talk about. I don't trust you, but I still crave you. You're like a fucking drug. I ought to stay away, but I can't."

I don't know what to do with his words, what to think. I don't know what to do with the fact that they send a thrill zinging through me.

"I wasn't looking for information. I swear it, Damian. I just wanted to talk to my—"

"You do not make the decisions here, Alina. We are not talking. We are fucking or I am leaving."

I wet my lips. His expression is hard, dangerous. He prowls closer until he looms over me. He lifts his hand. I flinch away before I realize that he only intended to sweep a strand of hair from my cheek.

His expression grows even harder, colder. I shiver and shrink away from him.

With a hiss, he takes my hands and pulls me to my feet. He presses his mouth to mine, not in the hard, punishing kiss I expect, but softly, gently.

Then he pulls back and drops my hands, his gaze locked on mine. He stands inches away, not touching me.

"Let me make something perfectly clear. I will pull your hair while I take you from behind because it turns us both on. I will smack that gorgeous ass until it's red and stinging because it turns us both on," he says, his voice like smoke, like gravel. "I will put my finger or my cock in your ass because it turns us both on. I will tie you up, make you beg because it turns us both on. I'll shove my cock in your mouth, down your throat, make you gag, make you cry, because it turns us both on. I'll throw you on the bed or the floor and fuck you senseless, because it turns us both on."

He pauses, his black-eyed gaze intense. "But I will never fucking raise a hand to you in anger. That's twice you've flinched from me in fear, Alina. Don't do it again."

I stare at him, my whole body shaking, every breath a panting rasp. Those things he said… I want him to do all that and more. I want his cock down my throat, his finger in my ass, his hand rough and strong as he spanks me. He is my drug as much as I am his.

"Do you understand?" he asks.

"Yes." I believe this man who is a criminal, a killer, the villain of the story when he says he will not raise his hand to me in anger.

"Good." He runs the pad of his thumb along my lower lip. "Now get in the bedroom, get these clothes off, and wait for me on your fucking knees."

Panting, I stare at him, my thoughts whirling. Then I turn and do as he ordered.

He doesn't follow me, not right away. He takes his time, letting me wait on my knees beside the bed, my clothes in a pile on the floor. My nipples are hard. My pussy is wet. I'm so turned on that it hurts.

I imagine him in the living room, looking out at the

lights, taking his time as he finishes his drink. And every second that ticks past just makes me want him more.

Finally, finally, he walks through the door. He takes his time, carefully hanging up his suit jacket after he slides it off. Pulling his shirt from his waistband then unbuttoning it as he stares down at me, baring his perfectly muscled, perfectly tattooed torso. My breathing is fast and shallow as he undoes his belt, his button, his zipper then skims his pants down his muscled thighs. His black boxers follow. Naked, he is unbelievably beautiful, his muscles long and corded, his shoulders wide, his waist and hips narrow. His cock juts forward, thick and hard.

In this moment, there is nothing I want more in this world than to take him in my mouth.

He comes to stand in front of me, towering over me.

"Open," he orders, and even that turns me on.

I open and he pushes the head of his cock into my mouth. He takes his time, sliding along my tongue, grabbing my hair and pulling so my head tips back as his cock moves deeper. I lick him and suck, greedy, wanting only to please him. He groans and the sound weaves through me. I am doing that to him. I am making him groan and pump his hips and suck in his breath.

Angling my head, I take him deeper. He's so big, so hard.

He moves, fucking my mouth, his cock stretching my lips, sliding to the back of my throat. I wrap my arms around his thighs as I take him as deep as I can. He groans, the sound twisting my lust even tighter. I want to touch myself, rub my clit, but I don't dare unless he tells me to. I hum against his cock and I can tell he approves.

"Fuck," he groans, pulling free of my mouth. "Get on the bed."

I do, crawling on all fours, looking back at him over my shoulder. His gaze is locked on my ass.

He grabs me around the waist and flips me face up, then kisses me, rough and hungry.

He slides on a condom, bends my knees and pushes them up, then shoves his cock inside me in a long, hard thrust. I'm tight, but so wet. I feel every inch of that thrust, every inch of his cock sinking into me.

He moves, pumping a rhythm that makes me writhe and moan.

His fingers dig into my thigh. My nails claw at his ass. This isn't sweet or gentle or soft. It's rough and hard and fast and I feel myself spiraling as his thrusts come faster.

"Come for me, Alina." The command combined with the sound of his voice drives me closer to the edge. His cock glides against my clit as he slides out, in. I break apart, my orgasm hard and fast, making me jerk and scream as he goes rigid above me, body taut, head thrown back as he comes.

I don't know how long I float, but I think it's a while before I finally come back to myself. When I do, Damian lies on his side beside me, watching me as he plays with my hair.

"You thirsty?" he asks.

I realize that I am and nod.

He gets up and comes back a minute later with two glasses of ice water. Pushing up to a sitting position, I take the glass from him and gulp half of it down then set it on the bedside table.

"You like boats?" he asks.

I blink, confused. "Boats? Like a sailboat?"

He tips his head to the side, studying me. "More of a motor boat."

"I've never been on a motorboat, but I like the beach and the ocean…"

He nods. "My brother wants you on the family boat."

"Your brother…the family boat…" I'm confused. Is he asking me? No, I think he's telling me. Unease skitters through me, though I can't say why. "Um, okay."

"Okay," he says, then gets up, gets dressed, and leaves.

And every evening at 8:00, he comes back and fucks me till I scream.

We don't talk that first night. He's too angry with me. But each night, his anger eases a little. He still won't talk about the night I called Markus, but we talk about other things. Our childhoods. High school. College. Politics. He tells me funny stories and I laugh until I cry. And I won't pretend I'm not secretly thrilled that he laughs at my stories, too.

"How did you get this scar?" I ask one night, tracing my fingers along the pale line on his lower back.

"Knife," he says. "Guy was aiming for my kidney. He wasn't fast enough."

I stare at him. "And this one?" I ask, touching the curved mark on his shoulder. The marks are old, healed, just thin white lines now.

"Also a knife," he says. "Different guy. Different fight."

I lean in and press my lips to the scar on his shoulder. Then I kiss the scar on his lower back. I kiss the one on his thigh.

He shifts so that my lips hover over his hard cock.

So I kiss that too.

Each night, he leaves me sated, exhausted. And each night, he leaves.

The fact that I crave his touch each day while he is gone is bad enough. The fact that I crave his company, his laughter, the way he looks at me when I talk, the way he shares little pieces of himself with me is even worse. I tell myself that sex with Damian is something I can walk away from when this is all over. It's harder to convince myself that I'll be able to walk away from his friendship.

Is that what it is? Friendship?

No. It isn't even a temporary friends with benefits arrangement. I am his captive, his collateral.

I *know* that. And I'm too smart to fall for Damian Russo, Mafia prince, criminal, killer.

Aren't I?

18

Alina

When Damian said a boat, I expected a boat.

This isn't a boat.

The thing is huge and sleek and like something out of a magazine or a fever dream. No sails, just clean lines, white and chrome and oozing piles upon piles of money. The kind of yacht I imagine Jeff Bezos or Elon Musk might own, parked alongside their rocket ships.

My steps falter as we approach it and I realize that this is where I'll be spending the weekend. But it isn't just the boat that's making me anxious.

It's the dynamic Damian and I have established.

I've come to crave his body. That doesn't mean I like it. I mean, I like Damian's body. A lot. A whole fucking lot. But how can I want someone like Damian Russo so much that I can barely sit still? He's like an addiction just lying under the surface of my skin. A want...a need...an addiction I can't control.

But it's only for a little while. This—whatever this is—isn't forever.

I keep telling myself that's a relief. But I'm having a hard time believing it.

I sigh. It's one thing to want his body. Quite another to want…something more.

"Problem?" Damian asks. He stands beside me wearing a white linen shirt, black pants and a pair of mirrored shades that hide his eyes. Beside him is Luca, holding true to his promise to accompany me on all field trips outside of the condo. He's been mostly silent, a stony statue in jeans and a polo, wearing his most professional persona. Or was the guy who ate ice cream with me on the balcony the persona, one designed to ferret out all the secrets Damian thinks I'm hiding?

Despite having spent time with each of them separately, I haven't really had a chance until now to see the two men together. He and Damian are clearly comfortable with each other, managing to have entire conversations with only a couple of words spoken between them.

"No problem," I mutter. "I just didn't realize that your family has more money than God."

This doesn't get a reaction from him—not a snort, not an acknowledgement of my delightful wit. Not that I expected such an acknowledgment. Whatever.

"We're late," is all he says in reply.

As if that's my fault.

The helicopter ride took longer than expected. The pilot said something about the wind.

When I'd seen the helicopter waiting for us on the roof of Harrah's, I'd been torn between demanding if it was safe and jumping up and down in excitement. I'd never been in a helicopter before. I'd glanced down at the strappy sandals I'd chosen to go along with my flowing hot pink maxi dress and wondered if I'd have to bend and run under the blades like they do in the movies. Turns out I did.

In moments, we were flying high above Vegas. The city gave way to sand. The sand gave way to red sandstone that, under the glare of the sun, looked like it was on fire. It felt like minutes, but was probably closer to a couple of hours before we reached the California coastline. We flew along the coast, with the sparkling blue Pacific Ocean next to us.

There was a car waiting when we landed, and it brought us here: The Marina at Dana Point. There are what look like thousands of boats in front of us—sailboats, motor boats, big boats, small boats—and behind us, cliffs rise toward the sky.

"The Luciana," Damian says.

"Pretty name," I say, as I stare at the ship with wide eyes.

"It was my mother's name."

I glance at Damian, struck by the whisper of soft emotion in his voice, but he's already walking away.

I know very little about Luciana Russo, other than the fact that she died.

"Beautiful, isn't she?" Luca says.

"Yes," I say, with a wary glance at Damian. He's been off, tense ever since we left the condo this morning and it's making me nervous. "Did you know her? Luciana Russo?"

"I did," Luca says, his expression hard to read. Wistful? Pensive? "She was kind to me when she had no reason to be."

I don't know what to say to that.

We board the floating hotel—Luca tells me the gangplank is actually called a passerelle—and I try my best to look like this is something I do all the time. That my eyes aren't drawn to every line, every detail, as I try to memorize it all since I know this will never happen again.

Which is a good thing, of course.

The helicopter, the yacht, they remind me that these possessions were purchased by criminals. That every foot of this ship is soaked in blood, in drugs, in unspeakable horrors I can't even imagine and don't want to.

Blood money.

These are not good people. They are villains.

Damian is a villain. He is the bad guy. He is the nightmare—the monster hiding under the bed.

And Luca, as amiable as he's been, helps that monster in ways I don't want to think about.

And my brother… I think my brother is part of this, too. Not at the level of Damian and Luca, but he's involved somehow. Markus didn't just play a few games of poker with Damian. He works for him. I know it in my gut. It would explain the texts that go back for years. It would explain why Damian trusted Markus to walk out of a room owing him a million dollars. They know each other. And that isn't a comforting thought.

At the end of the passerelle is a large basket. Damian and Luca slide off their shoes and put them in the basket. I watch, bemused.

"You need to take those off," Damian says, gesturing at my sandals.

"Off? Why?"

"High heels can damage the teak decks. We go barefoot or wear boat shoes. Non-marking soles. Wear these," he says and hands me a pair of beige crocheted mules with a triangle logo that reads: Prada Milano. I have a feeling these aren't knock-offs.

I slip off my sandals and slide on the mules. They fit perfectly.

I cut Damian a sidelong glance. "You…bought these for me?"

He smiles at me, his real smile, the one that crinkles the corners of his eyes. "Like them?"

I nod.

He leans close and whispers, "You're welcome."

"For an asshole, you're incredibly considerate," I say.

He laughs, the sound washing over me, making me smile.

Luca crosses to the far side of the open outdoor area at the back of the yacht where another man stands. They greet each other and quickly become engrossed in a conversation. I notice that the man has a gun tucked into his waistband.

I follow Damian across the wide deck that has a built-in, u-shaped outdoor seating area surrounding a hot tub. He holds the doors and gestures for me to precede him into a room that looks like something out of a fancy hotel. Long ivory sofas accented with pale, seafoam blue throw pillows face each other, separated by a narrow glass and chrome coffee table. There's a bar along one side of the room, manned by an actual bartender. Huge windows look out at the ocean.

In this room are three people, all of whom look in our direction as we enter. A man and two women.

The man rises from the sofa and approaches. He looks a little like Damian, but there's a harshness to his features. His jaw is more square, the hollows under his cheekbones more pronounced, his lower lip fuller than his upper. He wears his dark hair shorter than Damian does, and he's perfectly clean-shaven.

Leonardo Russo, Damian's older brother.

The head of the Russo family.

The boss. The current king.

"You must be Alina," Leo says to me, his words perfectly friendly, his tone less so. His gaze flicks over me like I'm something he scraped off the bottom of his shoe.

My chest tightens and a cold sweat breaks out on my skin.

"I must be," I agree.

"Leo, this is Alina Madsen," Damian says. "Alina, this is my brother Leo."

"Welcome," Leo says, the word as warm and welcoming as freezer burn. His eyes are dark, cold.

"Thank you."

It all feels incredibly awkward. Leo doesn't smile. Maybe he never smiles.

Damian isn't smiling either.

The brothers make a dynamic duo of intimidation.

Leo glances at the woman next to him. "One last thing, Nicole," he says. "I need you to coordinate a meeting this week regarding the cybersecurity initiatives." His tone is different with her. Polite. Professional.

"Of course, Mr. Russo," she says, rising as she closes the tablet she holds.

She has dark hair, scraped back into a tight bun. No makeup. Glasses with thick black frames, the lenses magnifying her eyes so she looks like a frightened owl. No jewellery. She's tall, but it's hard to determine what her figure looks like. Her shoulders are hunched, her neck jutting forward. She's wearing a beige drop-waist dress with ashy grey horizontal stripes. I could not imagine a less flattering combo of color and style if I tried.

"This is Nicole Milano," Damian says. "Leo's assistant."

She reaches her hand out to me without meeting my

eyes, instead looking somewhere over my left shoulder. Her nails are short and unpolished, the cuticles ragged. Her handshake has the strength of a stalk of celery that's been sitting at the back of the fridge for a month.

"Hello," she says, her fingers squeezing mine for a second, as if she's offering reassurance.

An ally, one who isn't related to the Russos.

"Hi, Nicole." I wonder what her story is. How she got this job. She just doesn't strike me as the person Leo Russo would hire as his EA. Then again, I don't know Leo Russo, so I ought to have no expectations about him. Maybe she has superhuman organizational skills.

"Enjoy your dinner," she says softly and turns to leave.

"Nicole," Leo says. She freezes. "You'll be joining us for dinner. My date was unexpectedly detained. I'll need you to round out the numbers."

"Of course, Mr. Russo."

There's another woman in the room, standing a few feet away. Her head is cocked as she studies me, her arms crossed over her chest.

I already know who she is. I've seen her in the news. Sabina Russo. She's twenty-three, same age as me. But there's an air of sophistication about her that I definitely don't possess. The news talked about her donating to worthy causes and hosting charity events—as if that somehow might absolve her of her family's business activities.

"This is my sister," Damian says, gesturing toward her. "Sabina."

Sabina is drop dead gorgeous. A cool kind of perfection. Her dark brown hair falls in a sleek curtain to her shoulders. Her chin is delicate and a little pointed. She has full lips, glossy red, and, unlike her brothers' dark irises, hers are a pale blue. A cool blue, like chips of ice. She's wearing an emerald green dress that I would bet all the pennies in my meager bank account costs more than I make in two months at the club. Her wedge heels are precariously high, but even with that help, her height only matches mine. I'm five-six, so that would make her....petite. Five feet one at the absolute most. Clearly, her brothers got the height in the family when it was being doled out.

Despite her slight stature, Sabina strikes me as every bit as intimidating as her older siblings.

"Alina," she says in a cool tone as she holds out her hand to me.

I hesitate only slightly before taking it. Her skin is smooth but as cool as her voice. She has long nails, painted gold. The length and perfect manicure could only be maintained by someone who doesn't do a lot of manual labor.

"Sabina," I say as calmly as I can. "It's nice to meet you."

"Yes," she agrees, her icy eyes narrowing. "So you're Damian's latest, are you?"

"Latest?"

"Girlfriend."

I laugh at this out loud before I can stop myself. "I'm not sure I'd use that word."

"Oh? What word would you use?"

I feel Damian's gaze on me, searing. I ignore it.

"I'm his prisoner," I say easily. "For the next few weeks, anyway."

Damian grunts, but I don't look his way. Nicole makes a choked sound.

"His prisoner," Sabina repeats coolly, "that he's brought on a family weekend."

"I can leave," I offer. "I don't want to get in the way."

"Alina has a way with words," Damian says stonily.

"I see that." Sabina's gaze grows even narrower, and she gives me a sweep from head to toe. "You're a bit of a smart-ass."

"I…can be," I admit uneasily.

She stares at me for what feels like a full minute, with absolute, deadly silence in the room. Even the bartender had stopped clinking glasses and bottles.

Finally, a smile spreads slowly across her face, transforming it from gorgeous to transcendently beautiful.

"I like you," she says. Then flicks a look at Damian. "I like her."

"Great," he replies. "Then all is well with the world."

She hooks her arm through mine. "We're going to be good friends."

"Are we?"

"We are. And you know how I know this?"

"How?"

She shrugs a shoulder. "Because I always get what I want."

"Always?"

"Yes. Always."

For some reason, I can't seem to summon any distaste for her. Her change of mood has actually transformed the entire ambiance of the room. She emanates good cheer. Sunshine and roses. I could use a fuckton of sunshine and roses in my life.

I like her, and that's…well, that's incredibly inconvenient.

"You two are late as fuck," she says with a mock stern glance at me. "Keeping my brother busy, are you?"

Her meaning isn't hard to decipher.

"As a bee," I quip.

She taps her perfectly manicured index finger against her lips. "Don't male bees die right after sex? Something about their tiny dicks and abdominal tissues being ripped out during intercourse…"

Any doubt I might have had about Sabina fitting right in with her ruthless brothers evaporates right there. "At least they die happy."

Nicole makes another choked sound. Either she's smothering a laugh, or I've horrified her twice in the span of a minute.

Luca chooses that moment to join us. He greets Sabina with a chuck under her chin, which she tolerates, Leo with a bro hug that Leo returns, and Nicole with a nod that she mirrors.

The exchange tells me a lot about Luca's position in the hierarchy. I thought he was Damian's minion, guarding me as ordered. But I remember now what he said the first time we met, that he works *with* Damian, not *for* him. And his interaction with Leo and Sabina makes him seem almost like family.

"We've held dinner until you got here," Sabina says. "But I'm starving so let's eat."

Her arm still hooked through mine, she draws me into an adjoining room. A round glass table is set with gold cutlery and plates that look like they were stolen from a five-star restaurant. An arrangement of colorful flowers adorns the center, low enough that diners can still see each other over top. Damian pulls out a seat, and stares at me. I take the hint and sit. Leo sits to my right, Nicole across from him. Luca sits to my left, next to Nicole, Damian beside her, Sabina across from me on Leo's right.

I feel uncomfortable, out of place, and I wish

Damian were beside me to make sure I don't use the wrong fork. There are three fucking forks. And three fucking knives. Four, if you count the butter knife.

I drain the glass of wine a steward pours for me within seconds. He refills it without hesitation.

Huh. I'll need to keep an eye on that. The last thing I want is to be falling down drunk while I eat dinner with the piranhas.

The appetizer is served, a Caprese salad with tomatoes, fresh mozzarella, basil, and a balsamic drizzle. I wait until Sabina chooses her utensils, then follow her lead.

Nicole leans over and whispers, "Pace yourself. There are seven courses."

We make our way through shrimp cocktail, lobster bisque, and a green salad before the main course is served. Filet mignon accompanied by garlic mashed potatoes and grilled asparagus. Luca and Sabina carry most of the conversation. Nicole keeps her eyes on her plate. Leo glowers, mostly at me.

Every time I glance at Damian, he's watching me, his expression intent.

I hadn't thought I was hungry, given my uneasy position in this den of criminals, but this meal is literally the most mouth-watering food I've ever been served in my life. It beats a bagful of grease from McD's, any day.

"So what do you do, Alina? When you aren't my brother's prisoner," Sabina asks with a lighthearted grin. Either she doesn't believe me or she doesn't care.

I don't really want to mention my time at the Emerald. I'm about to say I'm between jobs when Damian says, "She's a writer."

I swear there's a hint of pride in his voice.

"A writer?" Sabina claps her hands. "What have you written? Have you published anything?"

"An online magazine published one of my short stories," I say.

"You've been holding out on me," Luca says. "How did I not know this? What's the story about?"

Before I can answer, Damian says, "It's about a young woman who finds her mother's diary after her death. After reading it, she comes to view her mother as a person rather than a parent. Inspired by her new insights into her mother's resilience, she finds the courage to pursue her own dreams."

I feel like time freezes. He read my story. Damian read my story. And he got it. Got what I wanted to say. And he liked it. I can hear it in his voice.

"Wow," Sabina says softly.

"Wow," Luca repeats, eyebrows lifting. "I'm impressed."

A moment of silence follows before Leo asks Luca, "How's the restaurant coming along?"

"A few hiccups with licensing. Nothing Cassio and I can't handle." Innocuous words, but I can't help but suspect some form of bribery or coercion being involved in handling it.

"I had lunch with Dante yesterday," Sabina says.

"Liquid or otherwise?" Damian asks.

"A bit of both," Sabina says, her expression worried. "I think he's getting better…"

"Except on the days when he isn't," Leo says. "I'll speak with him."

He exchanges a look with Damian, one I can't read. But I don't need to ask what they're thinking or feeling. I know all about having a brother whose use of substances puts him in a very bad place.

Luca lightens the mood, launching into a story about his latest foray into online dating that makes everyone laugh, even pulling a short huff out of Leo and making Nicole smile into her plate.

For dessert, we have tiramisu. I've never had it before, but now I want to have it every day going forward. Forever and ever.

When the dishes are cleared away, and coffee is served, Sabina clinks her spoon against the side of her cup.

"I have a very important announcement to make," she says.

All attention in the room goes to her.

19

Alina

Sabina clears her throat, presses her hands against the surface of the table and rises to her feet. "It's good news."

Despite that claim, there's a shadow that's fallen across her lovely face and her forehead is a little furrowed. She takes a deep breath and lets it out slowly, shaking off whatever anxiety she seems to be experiencing. A smile spreads across her face. "I'm engaged."

There's no immediate reaction to this.

"I'm sorry," Damian says. "I must have heard you wrong. I thought you said you were engaged."

"I did say that."

"Engaged." He blinks. "To be married." His gaze flicks to her left hand. No ring.

"Yes." Sabina's chin kicks up a notch.

I glance at Leo who's regarding his sister like he's smelling something bad.

"To whom?" he asks.

"My boyfriend." She glares at her brother. "Roberto Costa. You met him at Christmas." She looks back and forth between Leo and Damian, both of whom regard her with stony expressions. "You *both* met him at Christmas." She looks at Luca, as if hoping for support. "You played pickleball with him."

"Yeah, and he sucked," Luca offers, then shrugs when she narrows her eyes at him. "Just telling it like it is."

"Roberto. The kid from college," Damian says.

"He isn't a kid. We've been together over a year."

"And now you're engaged," Leo says, frowning at her naked ring finger.

I feel a little sorry for Sabina while at the same time I am so grateful that he is turning his glower on someone other than me.

"That's right. I'm incredibly happy and I just wanted to share this amazing news with you all."

Clearly, this isn't amazing news for all present. And while I've only just met Sabina and don't pretend to know her, she doesn't actually sound incredibly happy. I glance at Nicole. She's frowning and chewing her lower lip.

Leo narrows his eyes. "He asked you without consulting me? Without speaking to the head of the family first?"

"He spoke with Papa at Christmas. He was just waiting for the right time to ask me." Sabina stares her brothers down, clearly unfazed by their less than enthusiastic reaction to her news.

Damian and Leo exchange a look. Leo offers the barest hint of a nod to his brother.

"Not going to happen," Damian says. "You'll marry this guy over my dead fucking body."

"What?" Sabina's voice turns sharp, those glacial blue eyes sliding from Damian to Leo.

"I don't know this guy. He could be anyone," Damian says.

"He's not anyone. He's the man I am going to marry."

I wonder at her choice of words. 'The man I am going to marry,' not 'the man I love.' Maybe I'm being nitpicky, but it seems like there is a world of difference between the two.

Leo scoffs. "Some random college student? Who is he? Who's his family?"

"What difference does his family make?" Sabina asks.

"You know it makes a fucking difference, Sabina," Damian says. "A big fucking difference."

Fire enters Sabina's ice-blue eyes. "Fuck you, Damiano. And that goes double for you, Leonardo."

I feel sorry for her. I've only ever had to contend with one brother, who has always been mostly a fuck-up, too busy trying to manage his own shit to be particularly interested in mine. I can't imagine having to contend with two controlling assholes like Leo and Damian. I wonder if the other two brothers are just as bad.

Sabina glares first at one brother, then the other. "The thing is, I'm not asking you for your permission. Papa already gave his. I'm letting you know. I'm sharing my good news with my family because I want you to be with me on my wedding day. I want you to accept Roberto into the family."

"I already have someone I've chosen for you," Leo says, his voice low and lethal. "Someone who'll be a far more useful match."

"*You've* chosen for me?" Sabina asks, her voice equally low and lethal.

Leo cocks his head. "Damian and I have already

discussed it at length. Cass and Dante are in agreement. It's done."

"This is the twenty-first century. You're seriously talking about an arranged marriage?" Sabina makes a dismissive wave.

"It's the perfect match," Leo says. "Right, Damian?"

"The perfect one," Damian agrees. "And it's your duty as the daughter of the late Salvatore Russo to agree to this."

"And who is this paragon, this perfect match?" Sabina asks, almost sounding bored, as if the answer doesn't really matter to her.

"Nikolai Ivanov," Damian says.

Sabina's eyes widen.

"Oh, hell no," she sputters. "Not in a million fucking years would I ever have anything to do with that loathsome piece of shit."

"You'll marry him next month," Leo says firmly. "You'll be a beautiful, and obedient bride to him."

"Very obedient," Damian agrees.

"Obedient? I'll throw myself off a building first. I'll jump overboard. I'll..." Sabina blinks. Her eyes narrow. "Wait. You're fucking with me. You're fucking with me, aren't you?"

There is a long silence, so quiet I can hear my heart pounding in my ears.

The next sound surprises me. Damian's laughter, a rich, full bodied sound that rumbles in his chest and echoes around the room, rhythmic and contagious. It sends a shiver of unexpected pleasure through me. The next moment, Leo and Luca join in, their laughter rolling like waves.

"You shitheads," Sabina says. "I hate all of you so fucking much."

She lets out a giggle. Then a snort. Then she goes all in, her laughter bright and sparkling, punctuated by the occasional wheeze or snort.

My lips twitch. I can't help it. Beside me, Nicole keeps her head down.

"Oh, that's right," Sabina says. "You three assholes go ahead and cackle like hyenas after you almost gave me a heart attack." She smacks Leo's arm. It only makes him laugh harder.

"As if anyone could make you do something you don't want to do," Luca says.

"But the look on your face," Leo says to his sister, his wide grin making him look like a different man than the one I met when I first arrived.

"Of course, we'll need to talk to the asshole first," Damian says after a moment.

"He is not an asshole," Sabina says primly.

"A long talk that he will not enjoy at all," Leo says. "But then, if that talk goes well....fuck. If Papa approved, then that's enough for me. We'll stop referring to him as the asshole and you can marry him. I'll even walk you down the damn aisle myself. Okay?"

Sabina runs to him and throws her arms around him, then does the same to Damian.

"I hate you both, but I love you so much!"

"Ditto," Damian tells her.

Luca watches the exchange with a wistful expression.

Nicole and I share a look, an incredulous one. This isn't our world. This is the world of the Russos, and we're just visiting.

Dinner winds down and we settle on the sofas for coffee and after-dinner drinks. Sabina excuses herself for a moment.

"Papa ever mention to you that Roberto asked for Sabina's hand?" Damian asks Leo.

"No, he did not." He takes a sip of brandy. "He say anything to you?"

"No, he did not," Damian replies. "I have to wonder..."

"As do I," Leo says.

I wonder what they're wondering, but I don't dare ask. A moment later, Sabina returns and Luca teases her about being too young to get engaged. The conversation turns to sports, then betting, and I feel like the words the three men use carry undercurrents I can't understand. I'm mostly quiet, observing. Every so often, I glance up to find Leo watching me with an expression of distaste.

I'm relieved when Damian finishes his drink, leans over and says, "Would you like a tour of the Luciana?"

"I would love a tour."

We bid the others good night and, taking my hand, Damian leads me out the double glass doors to the deck we crossed earlier.

"This is the aft deck." He gestures toward twin sets of stairs on either side of the deck. "Those lead down to the swim platform." I lean forward and catch a glimpse of a large platform with loungers, a table with a sunbrella, and two jet skis off to one side. "The room where we just had drinks is the saloon."

"Saloon," I say. "So not a living room."

"A living room that is called the saloon," he says.

"What about the room where we had dinner?"

"The dining room," he says.

"Okay, yeah, but what's it called on the Luciana?"

"The dining room," he says with a small smile.

I huff a laugh.

We take an outdoor walkway along the side of the

ship. It's lined with tall windows through which I see the saloon, the dining room, a staircase, an elevator. The air is warm, and there's a slight breeze. I pause to look at the night sky. It's very dark, the stars very bright. There are no city lights out here to dull the view of the heavens.

Damian stands behind me, he puts both hands on my upper arms, his palms warm against my naked skin.

"The last time I was on the Luciana was with my father," he says, and the sorrow in his voice guts me.

"Tell me about him."

He's quiet for a long moment, then he says, "He was a good father. Loving, kind, interested in the lives of his children. He was funny, loved a good joke."

I smile when he says that, thinking of what he and Leo just did to their sister. I guess the apples don't fall far from the tree.

"He liked to hear all sides of an argument before he made a decision, but once his decision was made, there was no changing his mind. He spoiled us, but also taught us the value of hard work, dedication, effort. Growing up, we had few rules, but those we did have were unbreakable. He always expected our best effort. If that made us come in first, great. But if our best earned a B or saw us come in last in a race or fumble the ball, he was still proud of us, so long as he knew we did our best."

"He sounds like a very good dad," I say softly. "Was he a good husband?"

"He loved my mother."

There's an undercurrent to those words, something Damian isn't saying.

"But..." I say.

Damian huffs a humorless laugh. "But he hurt her.

Not physically. He never raised a hand to her, never raised his voice to her. But he kept a mistress."

"Did she know?" I ask.

"She knew. We all knew. As a kid, I blamed his mistress, hated her for my mother's pain. As an adult, I understand she suffered too. And I blame only my father. He supported her, set her up in a nice place, gave her gifts and money. But he never loved her. Never gave her any real part of himself. She was just there, a convenience, because as my father explained, it's what men do."

We stand under the stars, Damian's warm hands on my skin. He pulls me against him, his chest to my back, his chin resting lightly on the top of my head, his arms wrapped around me. For a minute, I let myself pretend. Pretend that we are dating. Pretend that he cares about me. Pretend that there is a future for whatever this is between us. For a minute, I let myself recognize that I am drawn to more than just the physical, more than his looks, his body, the way he makes me feel with his hands and mouth and cock.

I am drawn to him, the whole package, and that is dangerous.

"He was a very good dad," he says after a time. "A great dad. A great man. But everyone has layers. He was often pulled away by the demands of the business. And sometimes, even if he was there physically, his mind was a million miles away." He pauses. "He raised Leo to take over, raised me to support my brother, to be his right hand. Raised my brothers to be part of the business."

"That couldn't have always been easy."

He laughs. "Sometimes, it pissed me the hell off. I couldn't fucking wait to get away, to go to college, to leave Vegas. Then, after four years away, newly minted business degree in hand, I couldn't wait to come home. I had all these ideas for the business, all these changes I wanted to implement."

"And your father didn't agree?"

"He didn't disagree. He just liked to hear all sides of the argument before he acted." He huffs a low laugh. "I didn't always come up on the winning side."

"Did you resent that?"

"Sometimes."

"But you loved him anyway."

"We had a complicated relationship.

"Yeah, I get that. But you loved him."

"I would have died for him. The night he was shot, I threw myself on him. It was instinct." He pauses. "But I wasn't fast enough."

If Damian had been fast enough, he wouldn't be here now. He would never have played poker with Markus, never taken me prisoner. It is so fucked up that the thought causes me pain.

"You were willing to die for him. That is a whole lot of love," I whisper.

He turns me in his arms until we face each other. His gaze meets mine. "You think someone like me is capable of love?"

The question throws me. "Family usually transcends love or hate and it's always complicated. It's on a different level. Blood is blood. My brother drives me crazy. He's a mess and a constant problem, but I love him with all my heart. And honestly? I'd kill for him."

He runs the backs of his fingers along my cheek. I can't help but lean into his touch, craving it. "Would you kill me?" he asks.

"In a heartbeat," I reply.

The night he took me prisoner, I would have meant

that statement with everything I am. Now…well, I'll just say that it's a good thing I'll never have to make the choice.

The reply doesn't anger him. In fact, he seems satisfied by it.

"To answer your question, yes, I loved my father," he says. "And sometimes I hated him. And I swear I'll find his killer and avenge his death and anyone who had a part in it." He turns away from me, toward the dark water. "*Anyone*," he says again. "And I'll do whatever it takes, step on whomever I have to, in order to get the answers I need."

The ice in his tone makes me shiver.

If he finds Enzo…if Enzo is guilty of this crime…if Enzo's still alive, Damian won't hesitate to take his revenge. I guess I'm pretty twisted, because I hope that I'd do the same, that if the guy who killed my parents was in front of me right now I'd have the balls to make him pay.

Damian turns back to me and searches my face as if trying to find some answer there.

"I shouldn't have brought you here," he says, shaking his head.

"I can leave," I offer instead of giving in to the instinct to ask why he shouldn't have brought me.

He snorts. "You think so, do you? We have a deal, Alina."

A deal. I'm his collateral until my brother pays up. The reminder hurts.

"And that deal is the only thing keeping me here," I say, my tone flat.

"The only thing?" He trails his fingertips along my upper arm.

"What else could there be?" I ask, and hate that I don't sound completely convincing.

"What else…?" Damian closes the distance between us in one step, pulling me to him and crushing his mouth against mine.

I don't resist, not for a single second.

20

Damian

I RUN my hand down Alina's back, my fingers sweeping along the tiny bumps of her spine. I cup her ass, her perfect, round ass as I kiss her. My blood burns. I want to be inside her. I want her soft and pliant beneath me. I want her screaming my name. I want to own her every thought, her every breath. What the fuck is wrong with me?

I take her hand and lead her to our stateroom. I open the door and draw her inside, flicking on the bedside lamp, bathing the room in a soft glow.

Alina trails a fingertip along the pale, sleek paneling of the wall, her gaze shifting to take in the view of the moonlit seascape through the panoramic windows.

"Wow," she whispers.

She turns to the bed and runs her palm over the silk duvet, then lifts one of the multitude of throw pillows and hugs it to her chest. Turning her head, she sends me a little smile over her shoulder as she opens a door to check out the walk-in closet and another to reveal the ensuite bathroom.

"I have something far more interesting for you to explore," I say.

"Oh?" She arches a brow and rakes her nails down my chest, my abdomen, hooking a finger in the waistband of my pants.

Pulling her against me, I kiss her. Her lips are lush and full, and the little whimper she makes is so fucking sexy.

"I want you naked," I say against her mouth, my hands gathering the flowing material of her dress, dragging it up her body, over her head. I step back and admire the way she looks standing there in her panties and bra. I turn her so her back is to me and unhook her bra, peeling it down her arms.

Her breathing speeds up.

I curl my fingers into the top of her panties and slide them down her legs, those endless, perfect legs, taking my time, skimming my fingers along her skin. I lift one foot then the other, pulling her panties free. Then I step back and walk a slow circle around her to admire the view.

"Fucking perfect, that's what you are," I say, my voice rough.

She wets her lips, swollen from my kisses, her gaze flashing to mine. Her pupils are dilated, her irises only a thin rim of blue. I stroke first one nipple, then the other, pink and swollen. Again, she makes that soft whimper.

Blood rushes to my cock. I'm hard as steel just looking at her.

I move to stand behind her, dragging my palm along the indent of her waist, the flare of her hip, the curve of her ass, her skin so soft and smooth.

Without warning, I spank her ass. She gasps and shifts foot to foot but makes no protest. My slap left a faint pink mark. *My* mark. A primitive part of me howls. *Mine*.

I imagine keeping her, never letting her go, tattooing my mark in her skin. Tattooing her mark in mine. My cock gets even harder.

Yeah, I'm a fucking Neanderthal.

I cup her breasts from behind, rolling her nipples between my thumb and forefinger, pinching them lightly, then harder. With a whimper, she arches into my touch and pushes her ass against my rock-hard cock, wriggling against me.

"Bad girl," I murmur and slap her ass again. She gasps but still doesn't protest. "You like that?" I ask, my lips against her ear.

"I don't know," she whispers, pauses, then says, "Maybe?"

I knead the swell of her ass and from the way she hums softly, I think her maybe might be leaning toward a yes.

I turn her to face me and kiss her lush mouth, her pale neck, the curve of her collarbone, then I lower my head, sucking first on one nipple, then the other, leaving them wet. I'm gentle, using almost no pressure. Then I suck harder, use my tongue, my teeth. Her fingers tangle in my hair, pulling me closer as she makes a low sound of pleasure.

That sound is like a velvet stroke on my cock.

I slide my fingers between her legs and find her wet and ready. Then, eyes locked on hers, I bring my fingers to her lips, push them into her mouth.

"Suck," I order. "Taste how much you want me."

She sucks and my cock presses against my zipper, so hard it hurts.

"I'm going to make you come with my tongue on your clit and my finger in your ass."

She makes an inarticulate sound, half whimper, half groan. I pull my fingers from her mouth.

"Would you like that, Alina?" I want no misunderstandings between us. I want to claim every part of her, own every part of her, and I want her consent. I want her to want it. I want her to need it, to need *me* like she needs air.

"Don't make me—" She shakes her head.

"Don't make you what? Don't make you do it? Don't make you want it? Don't make you say it?"

She wets her lips. "Don't make me say it."

"Oh, but you have to, pretty girl. It's the only way. Would you like my tongue on your clit and my finger in your ass, Alina?"

A heartbeat. Two. But of course I know the answer before she speaks. I've known her answer since the first second I saw her.

"Yes," she whispers, her voice low, the word torn from her.

My mouth crashes down on hers, my kiss rough, demanding, my tongue pushing past the seam of her lips. I lower her to the bed, my weight full atop her, my hips pinning her. She kisses me back, frantic, desperate, writhing beneath me, her hands tangled in my hair.

Then I kiss my way down her body, nipping her smooth skin, making her writhe.

I lift my head and watch her as I slide my palms up the insides of her thighs, forcing her legs wider. I kiss her belly, the inside of her thigh. The scent of her arousal twists my lust even tighter. I want to devour her, mark her, own her.

I slide my tongue along her wet folds, again, again,

my fingers splayed along her upper thighs, holding her still as she strains against my hold. Needing. Wanting.

The taste of her is like a drug as I lick and suck her clit.

She jerks and begs, the sound so fucking gorgeous. "Damian, please, please…"

I pin her hips with my forearm, holding her in place as I nip the inside of her thigh, then lick her to soothe the hurt. Then I lick up the centre of her cunt, again and again while she squirms and tangles her fingers in my hair.

With my free hand, I smear her moisture from her pussy to the crack of her ass, then press my finger against her asshole, pushing just the tip inside as I suck her clit. I slide my finger out, push it back in, my tongue stroking her clit. She thrusts her hips and gasps, low and breathy. Her heels press against the sheets, her whole body strung taut, as if my forearm pinning her hips is the only thing stopping her from fucking levitating.

Her body is my toy, my instrument, my clay.

I push my finger deep in her ass and I suck her clit hard. She screams, her whole body jerking, her muscles twitching and trembling as she comes.

I don't give her a chance to recover.

I climb her body and press my mouth to hers, her taste on my tongue and on her own.

I push my cock inside her, rough, hard. She wraps her legs around my back, her arms around my shoulders, her mouth eager as she returns my kiss, her body still pliant from her orgasm as I take her. Fuck her.

I am anything but gentle. Anything but giving. I take what I want, what I need, balls deep inside her.

Beneath me, I feel Alina start to come again, her

muscles tightening, her body spasming. With a roar, I let go, my orgasm crashing through me in an endless wave.

Finally, I roll to the side to keep from crushing her. She nuzzles against me, her face buried in the crook of my neck. Then she tips her head and looks up at me, her expression soft, open, full of trust, full of…affection.

No woman has ever looked at me like that. With good reason. I've never let a woman close enough for her to even consider it. I've never wanted to before.

I feel Alina's trust like a gut punch.

I brought her here so my brother can interrogate her. I brought her to the middle of the fucking ocean where the only thing that stands between her and harm is me.

I brought her because the head of my family ordered it.

Even worse, I brought her because, selfishly, I wanted her with me.

What the fuck is wrong with me?

21

Alina

I WAKE up and for a moment I don't know where the hell I am.

And then I remember. The yacht. The stateroom. Huge king-sized bed. Sleek, polished wood walls. Silk comforter. Butter-soft white sheets that are probably about a billion thread count. About a million throw pillows that are currently scattered all over the floor. I stretch, a smile curving my lips as I think about last night, about Damian.

Last night, just before I drifted off, the way he looked at me…

I roll to my side and reach for him only to find an empty bed. I'm alone. The fluffy pillow beside me is dented but vacant. It smells like him, like his warm skin, like citrus and spice. That scent is on me now, every inch of me, and it's threatening to sink deeper, right into my soul. I am in way too deep, barely treading water.

"What the fuck am I supposed to do now?" I mutter.

"Good question," a male voice answers.

I stiffen, then sit up, gathering the sheets to cover my naked body.

I was wrong. I'm not alone.

In the shadows of the room, I see a dark outline sitting in a chair, facing me. Watching me.

He rises to his feet and draws nearer, and I realize that it's Leo.

"Good morning," he says, his tone cold, boding nothing good.

"What are you doing in here?" I ask. Then hesitate, remembering whose boat this is. "Sorry for how rude that sounds, but I'm not used to waking up with a stranger watching me."

It's creepy, I think. *And weird. And deeply unsettling.*

"I'm not a stranger," he replies. "I'm Damian's brother."

"You're a stranger to me."

"You're not wrong," he acknowledges. "I have a few questions for you, Alina."

A shiver runs through me. I don't have to be Sherlock Holmes to deduce what Leo Russo wants to ask me.

"Where's Damian?" I ask.

"Not here."

"Where is he?" I press.

"He's not going to save you, Alina, if that's what you think," Leo says. He leans against the bedpost, his hands in the pockets of his black jeans.

"Do I need saving?" I ask as evenly and calmly as I can.

"That depends on your answers right now."

"I'm in bed."

"Yes, you are. So get up."

"I'm naked."

"Your point?" His gaze is as cold as a snake's.

"I don't think Damian would like you in here right now."

"Really. And why's that? You think he'd be jealous?" He scoffs. "Don't for one moment overestimate yourself, Alina. My brother doesn't give a steaming shit about you other than being his latest fuck."

My cheeks warm, partly from anger, partly from hurt. "Charming."

"Just telling the truth."

Is it? Am I just a fuck for the mafia prince who's made me crave him, made me care about him, despite my better judgment?

"I'm going to need you to leave so I can get dressed," I tell him firmly, "but I'm happy to answer any questions you might have for me later."

"You're fine the way you are," Leo says, and the way he looks at me chills my blood.

I want to tell him to fuck off, but fear freezes my tongue. I don't know him. All I know about Leo Russo is that he's the current boss—the dangerous head of the Russo syndicate, or whatever it's called.

If Damian is a demon, then that means Leo is Satan himself.

He could kill me, and I won't be able to do anything but scream. And it seems as if Damian will be no help to me. Maybe he left the room so Leo could have some one-on-one time with me. The possibility makes me both heartbroken and afraid.

"Get up," Leo says.

He has all the power. I have none. And he wants to make sure I know it.

"Get up now. Or I drag you to your feet."

I get to my feet, managing to keep the sheet around me, clutching it together at the chest. It's clear he wants me as vulnerable as possible. Frightened. Off balance.

Once I'm standing, he settles back into the chair he was sitting in when I woke up. He stares at me as I stand there, awkward, afraid.

I wait.

"I want to tell you a story," he says. "When I was nineteen, my father had me confront a man we suspected of spying. I asked him questions. He gave me answers. I didn't like his answers. I asked him if he was right handed or left. He told me right. So I took a knife and starting with his right little finger, I sliced off a bit of finger for each answer I didn't like."

He grabs my wrist and pinches the end of my right little finger to the furthest knuckle with his left thumb and index finger. Then he pinches the next knuckle and the next. "I kept slicing." He pinches the end of my right ring finger. "He never did give me an answer I liked."

I shiver as he moves along my right ring finger, pinching each section in turn, then starts on my middle finger.

He lifts his eyes to mine, dark, soulless. His expression is ruthlessly neutral.

Then he reaches into his pocket and pulls out a small box. It's black, tooled leather with a gold clasp. "A souvenir," he says, using his thumb to slide the clasp free then flip open the lid of the box.

There are ivory beads inside.

Except they aren't beads at all.

They're little bones. Ivory bones.

I feel sick.

He sets the box down on the low table beside him, then lifts a knife with a long blade.

"See this curve?" he asks, turning the knife. "It's

good for skinning. And this handle? Textured rubber so my grip doesn't slip, even in wet conditions." His smile is terrifying. "Things sometimes get a little bloody." He leans back in his chair, balancing the knife with his right index finger on the hilt and his left index finger on the tip of the blade. He stares at me, saying nothing.

Bile burns the back of my throat. Fear tightens my chest, my breathing shallow.

"Tell me about yourself," he says at last, silky smooth and full of threat, like a snake gliding through grass.

"You already know who I am."

He nods. "Alina Madsen. Cocktail waitress. Twenty-three years old. Sister of Markus Madsen. Girlfriend of Enzo Bianchi." He says the last words like he's spitting poison.

"Not an impressive bio, I'll admit it," I say. "And I am not Enzo's girlfriend. I dated him. He wouldn't take the hint when I no longer wanted to date him."

"Girlfriend of Enzo fucking Bianchi," he repeats softly.

"Do you label every woman you've ever dated as your girlfriend?" I snap and instantly regret it.

His eyes narrow.

"I don't know where Enzo is," I say to him. "I already told Damian this."

"Yeah, but the difference between me and my brother is that I know you're lying. Which is why I told him to bring you here this weekend. Miles out at sea… do you know what happens to pretty little liars who get in the way of me and the information I want?"

I clutch the sheet with both hands, trying to still their trembling.

Now everything makes much more sense. Me being here was Leo's idea, not Damian's. Of course. I sensed that something was off when he first mentioned the boat. I sensed he wasn't *asking*.

"If there was a lie detector here, I'd take it," I say. "Because I'm telling you the truth."

"I'm the fucking lie detector." Leo sets the knife down on the table. He rises and draws closer and it's all I can do not to cower away from him.

"I don't know where he is," I spit the words out, managing to sound more angry than frightened. "If I did, I'd tell you."

"Not that loyal to your so-called ex?"

"No, I'm not."

"You'd throw him under the bus to save your own ass?"

"I'd throw him under the bus because he deserves it. He's a bad guy."

Leo laughs at that, the sound dark and forbidding. "A bad guy." He shakes his head. "Tell me about his job. Who does he work for?"

I know I should come clean now, tell him what I overheard and my suspicion Enzo works for the Ivanovs. But I also know that's a monumentally bad idea. Leo will probably think I kept the information secret all this time in order to protect Enzo. Shit. I should have told Damian the truth right from the start. Why did I think that keeping this secret was a good idea, one that might save me and Markus at some point? If anything, revealing it now will seal my fate. Leo will drop me in the ocean without a second thought.

"He never talked about work with me."

"No?" He sweeps his gaze over me and I'm not sure if he's disgusted by what he sees or impressed. "I'm guessing he didn't trust you either."

"I don't know anything," I say, raising my chin.

Leo's lips curl to one side in a cruel smile. He takes another step closer, looming over me. "Here's something I know about people, Alina. Everybody lies. About small things, about big things. Sometimes it's easy to tell who's telling the big lies, sometimes it's not. At least, not until some duress is applied."

I stop breathing for a moment. My gaze snaps to the table and the knife and the box with its macabre contents.

He laughs and it's a bone chilling sound. "That's a bit extreme at this stage. There are other ways of extracting information from a reluctant mouth. Some ways don't even leave a mark. No evidence of what happened to get to the truth." He nods. "Others do. They leave marks and scars and are accompanied by a great deal of pain."

"I'm telling you the truth." My heart is pounding. A lump of terror sits in my throat.

"I doubt you are. But I will know for certain soon enough. See, I don't think it adds up. A new woman, out of the blue, lands in my brother's bed. And she happens to be the girlfriend of the fucker who took out my father—"

"I am not Enzo's fucking girlfriend," I grit out.

"She steals my brother's phone," he continues as if I hadn't spoken. "Searches for information. Installs spyware—"

"What? I never—"

"Sit down, Alina." He nods at the chair he'd previously been sitting in.

I shake my head vigorously, backing away. I don't get far. The backs of my knees hit the bed. I glance at the door, hoping for rescue. But there is no one to rescue me. Damian won't save me from his brother. He brought me here on his brother's orders, left me here alone to be interrogated by someone with a portable collection of his victim's bones.

Leo takes another step forward. There is nowhere left for me to go.

"I'm thinking this is a new situation for you. So, let's make this crystal clear," he says. "When I tell you to do something, you fucking do it. Now sit."

I stand, frozen by fear. When I don't move quickly enough, Leo reaches forward, grabs my arm, and tosses me like a ragdoll down into the chair. I stare up at him, clutching the sheet like it's my lifeline.

"Now, let's start over Alina. Where is Enzo Bianchi?"

"I don't know."

"Who does he work for?"

"I don't know."

"What did you tell Bianchi when you used my brother's phone to contact him?"

"What? No! I only called my brother!"

He makes a tsking sound. "Don't lie to me, Alina. This won't go well for you."

I stare up at him. Every cell in my body wants to cower, but I won't let myself. I won't give him the satisfaction. I glare at him, gritting my teeth.

"Do you think your show of bravery will convince me?" he asks, whisper soft, as he leans close, his black eyes blazing. "You work for the Ivanovs. I know it, you know it. Now I only need you to admit it out loud."

My eyes widen. He doesn't just think I'm involved because I dated Enzo. He actually thinks I work for the Ivanovs. "You think I'm a spy? I'm not a fucking spy! I...I dated Enzo for a couple of months, but I'm not a spy for anyone!"

"Maybe. Maybe not."

His smile is chilling as he rests his hand around my throat, thumb on one side, fingers on the other. I hold his gaze, my fingers twisting in the sheet, as if covering my nakedness will save me.

"Where. Is. Bianchi?" He growls.

"I don't know."

He nods as if approving my answer, but his grip tightens ever so slightly.

My heart slams against my ribs. I try to wriggle away, but he shifts forward, crowding me against the seat back.

"Who does Bianchi work for?"

"I don't know." The words come out on a rasp as he tightens his hold even more.

"And who do *you* work for, Alina Madsen?"

His grip grows tighter, tighter…

I let go of the sheet and scrabble at his hands, but my nails are short, and I can't even manage to scratch him. I can't breathe, I can't think. The world starts to go dark at the edges.

I'm not a spy!

I try to speak, but I can't form any words, just pathetic gurgles.

And then Leo suddenly pulls back from me, and I gasp and sputter and try to find my breath again. My hands are at my throat, protective, as if I could ward off another attack. I'm shaking, my head spinning. I think I might throw up.

Then I realize that Leo didn't let me go by choice.

Damian shoves his brother against the wall so hard that his head snaps back and slams against the gleaming pale wood paneling. He presses his forearm against Leo's upper chest, pinning him to the wall. They're about the same height, same size. But Damian has rage on his side.

"What the fuck are you doing to her?" he snarls.

Leo slaps Damian's arm away and jabs his finger in my direction. "You're blind. You know that? She's a goddamn spy!"

Damian's dark eyes flick to me, but only for an instant. "So you were going to fucking kill her?"

"I was questioning her."

They glare at each other, and I feel like they're having an entire silent conversation.

"The cops went to the warehouse," Leo says. "Strange how they got an anonymous tip. Lucky that Luca was thorough."

"She didn't fucking know anything about the warehouse," Damian says.

"She went through your phone. You have no idea what she knows."

"There was nothing on my phone to find," Damian says. "Just like there would be nothing on your phone. On any of the family's phones. You take me for a fucking moron?"

I'm shaking so hard that I know my legs won't hold me if I try to stand and flee the suite. Besides, where would I flee to? There is nowhere to run. So I shrink back in the chair and try to make myself as small as possible.

"I want Bianchi," Leo snarls.

"You think I don't?" Damian snarls right back.

"Then we are in agreement," Leo says, his dark gaze flicking to me. "Let's get some answers."

"You will not fucking touch her," Damian says. "You hear me?"

"Who's going to stop me?"

"I am."

With that, Damian physically drags Leo out of the cabin as I watch with shock.

It takes me a moment to gather myself, to drag on panties and bra and the pink dress I wore yesterday, to decide if I should stay put or follow. In the end, I follow, reaching the aft deck just as, with a roar, Damian wrestles Leo down.

22

Damian

FAMILY FIRST. Always.

That loyalty is branded on my soul, steeped in my bones and tissues. I was born to this code, raised to honor it, and I know no other way.

But as I slapped open the door to the stateroom and found Leo with his hand around Alina's throat, there was only one thing that mattered. Protecting her. Keeping her safe. Even if I had to stand against my brother to do it.

I'd wanted to comfort Alina, to sweep her in my arms and cradle her against me and swear no one would ever hurt her again. I'd wanted to pound my brother senseless for daring to put his hands on her.

Instead, I'd tried reason. I'd offered words and logic scraped from my tangled, twisted thoughts. Thoughts of breaking his fingers one at a time for touching her.

Leo wasn't interested in words or logic.

Problem is, Leo isn't just my brother. He is the head of our family, our organization. In all my life, I never imagined a moment where I would stand against him.

But that moment is now. Here.

For Alina.

My rage and righteous fury lend me the advantage as I drag my brother to the aft deck. I don't actually plan to take him there, I just move, wanting him as far from Alina as he can be. Short of pushing him into the ocean, this is it.

"What the fuck is wrong with you?" Leo snarls. "She's no one. Nothing."

She is everything.

We wrestle as we haven't in years, chests heaving, muscles straining.

I go down on one knee, surging forward, head up, back straight, hips close to Leo's leg as I lock my arms behind his knee. Pushing forward with my back leg, I drive myself back onto my feet, hauling Leo's leg up as I move. I keep moving forward, forcing Leo back, forcing him off balance until he goes down. With a roar, I fall on him, my fists thudding against his flesh.

23

Alina

I WATCH in horror as the brothers pummel each other, a flurry of fists, grunts, and curses. Leo lands an elbow strike to Damian's temple. I gasp, certain the bone will break under the force of the blow. Damian responds with a straight punch to Leo's throat.

They're going to kill each other. Because of me.

Frantic, I look around for help and find Luca standing against the railing with his arms crossed over his massive chest, his expression unreadable as he watches the two men fight.

"Do something!" I yell, grabbing his forearm and tugging.

"What would you like me to do?" he asks, his expression impassive. My efforts to move him are about as successful as me trying to lift a truck.

"Stop them," I say as Leo rolls and pins Damian. "He's going to hurt him."

"If by 'he' you mean Leo and by 'him' you mean Damian, then yeah, he's going to hurt him. But Damian's going to hurt Leo, too. It's kind of a two-way street with these two. That whole sibling thing." He shrugs. "I'm glad I'm an only child."

I stare at him, not sure what I'm supposed to say to that.

He rubs one side of his jaw. "They haven't gone at it like this in years. Probably at least a decade." His hazel eyes pin me. "Something big must have set them off. Any idea what that might be?"

"Unresolved childhood conflict?" I snap as Damian punches his brother in the gut.

"That's probably part of it," Luca says, extending his arm to block the path of another man who tries to move past him toward the fight. He turns his head and says, "Do not interfere."

The man nods and takes a step back, his expression deferential. Then he catches the back of one of the lounge chairs on the aft deck, steadying himself as he sways. Luca gives him a questioning look but says nothing before turning his attention back to the fight.

In that moment, I realize something. Despite the fact that he was treated like family at last night's dinner, I thought Luca was just one of Damian's bodyguards, someone unimportant in their organization. But as I see the look on the man's face, read his body language, I realize that Luca is someone with power in the Russo hierarchy. Someone who garners fear and respect.

And I realize something else. Despite his banter, Luca is tense. Worried.

"Go. This is private business between brothers," Luca tells the man, and he goes, his gait a little off, like he's trying to keep his balance.

I stand beside Luca watching Damian and his brother fight, trembling with a horrible mix of emotions. Leo could have killed me.

I thought Damian left me alone so his brother could do just that. But he didn't. He came for me. He's fighting for me. And while I hate the violence, the blood, the thud of fists hitting flesh, I'm secretly glad that he cares enough to fight for me. That makes me a terrible person. Doesn't it?

With a roar, Damian hauls Leo to his feet and slams him against the railing.

Something—no *someone*—tears past me. Sabina.

"Stop!" she yells. "Stop!"

She throws herself into the melee. Terror seizes me. They're going to hurt her. She's so tiny compared to them.

I run forward, drawing up short as Luca catches me around the waist and hauls me back.

"Do not interfere," he says, his tone flat and cold.

"I'm not—" I can't catch my breath. "I don't—"

I realize I'm crying, great gulping sobs shaking my frame. I force myself to slow my breathing the way the therapist taught me after Mom and Dad died. Box breaths. Inhale for a slow count of four, hold for a slow count of four. Exhale for a slow count of four. Hold for a slow count of four. I do it again. And again. My pulse slows. My thoughts become less chaotic.

I'm dimly aware of a sound, growing louder. An engine. A motor boat?

Luca lets go of me and turns. Then he freezes, closing his eyes, pinching the bridge of his nose between his thumb and forefinger while he sways back and forth.

"Luca?" I say. Is he seasick?

He doesn't answer. He turns toward the stairs that lead to the swim platform below. He holds the rails with both hands for a second, swaying, then he quickly descends.

My attention snaps back to Damian and Leo.

"What is wrong with you?" Sabina yells at her brothers, arms outstretched to either side, touching neither man, yet somehow holding them apart. They stand glaring at each other, faces and knuckles bloody, chests heaving. "You're acting like children!"

"He hurt her," Damian rasps, never taking his eyes from his brother. "He fucking touched what is *mine*!"

The word grabs hold of my heart and twists. Does he see me as a possession? As the collateral for my brother's debt? Or does he mean something else entirely?

"Yours?" Leo snarls. "She's working for the Ivanovs."

Sabina whirls and stares at me, her pale blue eyes locked on mine.

"You have no proof," Damian says.

"That was the point of my conversation with her," Leo says. "Getting proof. Or a confession."

"It wasn't a fucking conversation," Damian counters. "You were strangling her."

"What the hell is wrong with you, Damiano?" Leo asks. "Our techniques might differ, but you've used a similar approach many a time in the past."

"I—"

Damian's answer is cut short, his gaze locking on something behind me, his expression one of horror for a spare instant before it locks down.

I turn. Luca stands just behind me, knuckles white where he clutches the handrail. For an instant, I don't understand what I'm seeing, and then I do. Blood drips down the side of his face and onto the collar and shoulder of his pale blue polo shirt, staining it red. Then his lids flicker closed and he keels forward, dropping like a felled tree.

"Luca!" Instinct makes me reach for him, as if I can

somehow catch his massive frame or stop his fall. All I succeed in doing is getting myself taken down by his weight, pinned beneath him to the deck as rapid footsteps pound up the stairs then storm past me.

Men. Six of them. And they all have guns.

24

Alina

Damian starts toward me where I lie trapped beneath Luca's weight.

"Don't move," one of the gunmen says, his weapon trained on Damian, who catches my eye and offers a tiny shake of his head.

It doesn't take a genius to realize he wants me to stay still, stay quiet. Play dead. I'm now covered in Luca's blood, so I could probably pass for dead at a quick glance. Another gunman has his weapon aimed at Leo, who has pulled Sabina to stand behind him.

Frantic, I look around for any of the men I've seen standing in the shadows since I first arrived on the yacht, unobtrusive. Where the fuck are the guards?

The gunmen don't even glance my way.

I try to listen for Luca's breathing, for his heartbeat, but I'm at the wrong angle to hear anything.

He's been my guard, my jailor, and I know he is definitely not a good guy. But he's been kind to me. Bought me ice cream. Made me laugh. Talked to me. I don't want him to be dead.

Moving slowly so as not to attract attention, I slide my hand up his neck and almost cry when I find a pulse. He's alive.

"What the fuck is this?" Leo snarls.

The first gunman, a blond, motions with his gun. "Down the stairs." He has an accent. Russian?

"Fuck you."

The man grabs Sabina and yanks her in front of him, the muzzle of his weapon pressed to her temple. My heart lurches.

"Down the stairs, all of you," he says, and juts his chin toward one of the staircases that lead down to the swim deck. "I am not here to kill her, but I will if you force my hand."

Sabina's expression is cool and composed, as if having a gun at her temple is an everyday occurrence.

"Mikhail sent you," Damian says. "He plans to start a war?"

My gut tells that while he actually does care about who sent these men, he's talking mostly to buy time, trying to come up with a solution.

"Don't know any Mikhail," the gunman says. "Now, walk."

I hold my breath and stay perfectly still as they descend the stairs, the blond holding Sabina, his gun pressed to her temple. He's followed by Damian, who is followed by a second gunman who holds his weapon to the base of Damian's skull. A third gunman holds his weapon to the base of Leo's skull. The other men bring up the rear.

Once they're down the stairs and out of sight, I wriggle from beneath Luca's dead weight and crawl to the edge of the closest staircase, my heart pounding so hard I feel sick. Lying flat, I peer over the edge.

Below me on the swim deck, the blond holds Sabina off to one side, his gun still at her temple. Damian and Leo stand on the far side of the platform, backs to the ocean, the other gunmen aiming their weapons at them. A large motor boat floats off to one side. I hear the waves lapping at the sides.

"What did you do to my men?" Leo asks.

"They're fine," a woman's voice says. "Fast asleep. It was easy enough to distract the chef this morning and put something into their breakfast. After all, everyone trusts Leo Russo's assistant, don't they?"

For a second, I don't know who's speaking, and then I do.

Nicole moves to stand in front of Leo. Her hair is scraped back in its tight bun, her body covered by a horrifically ugly, oversized sac of a greenish brown dress. But something about her is different. Her posture? The tilt of her head? The timber of her voice?

I remember that both Luca and the guy who wanted to intervene in the fight between Damian and Leo seemed woozy, dizzy. They must have been drugged.

"Guess you found your spy, Leo," Damian says, sounding bored.

"What the actual fuck…" Leo's attention is fixed on Nicole. "How long have you been working for the Ivanovs, Nicole?"

"I don't work for them. This isn't about your war with the Ivanovs," she says.

"You betrayed my father," Leo says, his voice low, even. "You worked at his side for almost two years. You celebrated holidays with my family. You were invited to my cousin's baby's christening. And all along you were a spy for the enemy. You repaid my father by collaborating in his murder."

Nicole's chin kicks up a notch. "Sorry to disappoint, but I knew nothing about the hit on him until I heard about it with everyone else after he was dead. Saw it on the news. Too bad, really. It would have been an eye for an eye."

Leo stares at her for a long moment. I would expect his expression to be one of anger, hate. But he looks at her with a calculating gleam, as if he's sizing her up. "What the fuck are you talking about, an eye for an eye?"

"This is all because of what you did to my father. Killing yours would have been sweet justice. Instead, it seems I'll have to settle for killing you."

"I've killed a lot of people," Leo says, sounding bored. "You'll have to remind me who your father was."

She jerks as if he slapped her. Then she glances around the swim deck before turning to the blond gunman. "Where's the other woman?"

"What other woman?" he asks.

I shrink back, holding my breath.

Nicole looks at Damian. "Where's Alina?"

"She got up early this morning and grabbed some breakfast," Damian says. "Then she fell asleep again. Out cold in our stateroom. She must have eaten whatever you used to drug the guards."

There are men holding guns on him, on his brother, his sister, and he's lying to keep me safe. He's a good liar. His gaze doesn't so much as flicker.

Nicole nods. "It's unfortunate that she'll wake up to this mess, but I think she's a tough one. She'll survive."

She's not wrong. I am a tough one and survival is my specialty.

I crawl silently back to Luca's side. I noticed that neither Leo nor Damian carry a gun while they're on the boat, but the guards do, so maybe…

I exhale in a rush. There it is. Luca's Glock, tucked nice and comfy at the base of his spine. I pull it free and do a quick press check to confirm there's a round in the chamber. Then I wriggle back to my vantage point, calculating odds and angles.

There are six gunmen. One has his weapon on Sabina. Five have their weapons on Damian and Leo. As far as I can tell, Nicole is unarmed.

I swallow, adrenaline pounding through me. I have years of experience at the gun range, aiming at paper targets. But I've never shot a person. I don't know if I can. And which person am I supposed to shoot? How many can I take down before *they* shoot *me*?

The blond presses his fingers to his ear. He turns to Nicole. "Our lookout says that Russo's men have been alerted. Some sort of silent alarm. They are on their way. We need to go."

"Nicole—" Leo says.

"Shut up!" She whirls on him. "This is your fucking fault. Own it. You're responsible for the bomb that set all of this into motion."

Leo shrugs. "Probably wasn't me. I'm not really an explosives type of guy. I prefer things up close and personal."

"I'll give you up close and personal," Nicole snarls. "On your knees. Now."

Leo just stares at her, unmoving.

One of the gunmen moves forward and kicks Leo's legs out from under him while another forces him to his knees.

Damian surges toward his brother. A third gunman moves between them, weapon poised. Two others grab Damian's arms, holding him back.

"Today's not about you," Nicole says to Damian. "I

have no good reason to kill you or her." She tips her head toward Sabina. "So don't give me one."

"Damiano," Leo says. Damian shoots him a look, then pulls free of the two men holding him.

The pain on Damian's face reaches inside me and twists.

I would do anything to save my brother.

I have no doubt Damian feels the same. Sabina too.

"Today, you pay the price for what you did," Nicole says to Leo.

"I didn't kill your father."

Nicole ignores him and gestures to one of her men to hand her his weapon.

"Stop! No, don't do this! Please!" Sabina yells, struggling against her captor, trying to get to her brother.

"Sabina," Leo says, his tone one of command. "You will stay calm. You will let this happen. And you and Damian will live."

Even facing death, Leonardo Russo has an air of command, of confidence. And he puts family first. His brother. His sister.

But if he expects that little speech to calm Sabina, he is sorely mistaken. She struggles even harder, twisting and biting, a flurry of elbow jabs and stomps and kicks. Howling at the top of her lungs.

In that second, Damian tackles one of the guards, catching the man's wrists and struggling for the gun.

Everything happens in a blur.

Nicole aims at Leo.

Leo holds her gaze, his chin lifted. His jaw tense. "Do it," he snarls.

I aim at her, feeling sick, my hand shaking. Can I shoot this woman to save a man who'd just tried to strangle me?

After what feels like forever, Nicole lets out an anguished yell and drops her arm.

Whatever stopped her, the blond gunman feels no such hesitation. He shoots just as Leo surges to his feet. His body jerks and he spins off the edge of the swim platform, falling into the waves.

The blond grabs Nicole and shoves her toward the motorboat. "We need to go!"

"Leo," Sabina yells, struggling against the man who holds her. "Leo!"

But Leo is gone, sinking beneath the surface.

Sabina knees the gunman holding her in the groin, then stomps his foot, all while struggling and trying to elbow him in the gut. With a snarl, he punches her in the side of the head. As she falls to her knees, he hits her again with the butt of his gun and runs for the motorboat.

The blond turns and aims. At Damian.

My fear and anxiety fade. I have only one focus. In that instant, I realize that I can, in fact, shoot a person. And I do.

The blond jerks and spins, then falls to the deck.

I hear the roar of a second motor and see a boatload of men speeding toward us.

The remaining gunmen race for the boat that brought them, leaping across the distance as the motor revs. Their boat speeds away.

"Leo!" Sabina yells, struggling to her feet and staggering to the spot where Leo went into the water. She crumples to her knees.

"Get his gun," Damian orders, then dives into the waves.

Sabina crawls to where the blond gunman lies and

grabs his weapon. He doesn't move. I don't know if I killed him. And I don't know what to feel if I did.

Seconds crawl by with no sign of Leo. Damian surfaces for air then dives again.

I glance down at my flowy sundress. It will be dead weight in the water. I set down the gun and peel off my dress. Then I run down the stairs and dive off the swim deck into the cold ocean.

An hour ago—was it only an hour ago?—Leonardo Russo threatened me with a knife, strangled me until I blacked out, and I'm am fairly certain he would have killed me.

But he's Damian's brother and Damian loves him.

Losing his father gutted him.

I don't want him to have to grieve another person he loves. I don't want him to suffer. I can't bear it if he suffers.

I surface and gasp another lungful of air, then dive again. As the water closes over me, I realize just how dangerously deep I've fallen.

25

Damian

"ALINA!" I roar, treading water, searching the surface. What the fuck is she doing in the water? I'm torn between searching for Leo and searching for her. "Leo!"

"Damian," Sabina calls to me from the swim deck. "He's here. Leo's here. He's safe."

I glance over and see my brother pulling himself from the water. He staggers to his feet, his clothing drenched, a bloodstain stretching down his right pant leg. Behind him is Luca, his hair matted and bloody. But they're both alive and upright. I'll take it.

I scan the surface of the water. "Alina!" Where did I last see her? Where did she go down? "Alina!"

"Here," she says surfacing in front of me, breathing hard. "I can't find him, Damian. I'm so sorry. I can't find him."

I don't waste breath on words. I grab her and yank her to me, dragging her through the water toward the swim deck. Leo reaches down and offers his hand as I push her toward him.

She looks startled for a second, but takes his hand, then clambers up the ladder. I follow.

"Leo," I snarl at my brother as I climb the ladder to the swim platform, tamping down the emotions that threaten to swamp me. Anger. Fear. Joy. Relief. Too many feelings to tease apart and name.

"You must be pissed that I saved myself," he says, ruffling my hair like I'm a five-year-old. "You wanted all the glory, right?"

His words are light, but his expression is anything but.

Sabina throws herself against me and I pull her close in a one-armed embrace, but my eyes are on Alina where she stands to one side, hugging herself. She shot a man to protect me. She dove into the ocean to save my brother, the man who only this morning threatened to kill her, put his hands around her throat, strangled her.

She stands in only her bra and panties, her blond hair wet and tangled, her body shaking.

For an instant, we stare at each other, saying nothing.

Then I set my sister aside and yank Alina against me. My mouth is on hers before I can even think about it. She sags against me and I scoop her in my arms. Without another word, I carry her to our stateroom, cradling her against me.

I slam the door behind me and carry her to the shower, turning on the water and stepping under the pounding, hot stream with her. But I don't let go of her. I hold her against my heart, half afraid that if I let her go even for a second she'll disappear.

"What the fuck, Alina?" My voice comes out in a growl.

"Can you be more specific?" she whispers.

"What the fuck were you thinking diving into the fucking ocean?"

"High school swim team. I was probably safer in that ocean than you were." She tips her head back and holds my gaze, defiant.

I just glare at her, the water pounding down on us, my entire body vibrating.

Her long hair hangs in wet straggles over her shoulders and down her back. Last night's mascara leaves dark smears under her eyes. I've ever seen a more beautiful woman in my entire fucking life.

She huffs a sharp exhale. "I was thinking that your brother was going to drown. That I couldn't bear for you to suffer that, to know the pain of losing another person you love."

Her words make my chest feel tight, make it hard to pull a full breath. "And the gun?"

She frowns, looking confused, then her expression clears. "Luca's gun?"

"Yes, Luca's gun. You handled it like an expert."

"Not an expert," she says. "I'm out of practice."

"Practice," I say, harsher than I intend. "How much practice have you had?"

"Me, Markus, and Dad at the gun range every week from the time I was twelve until I left for college. It was Dad's version of family game night."

I wonder how my people missed that fascinating bit of information when they did their work-up on Alina.

"So you've shot paper targets at the gun range. Ever shot a man before?"

She shakes her head.

"Yet you shot a man today. To save me. Then you dove into the ocean to save my brother. The brother who tried to kill you."

"W-W-Well, I think if he really wanted to kill me, I'd be dead. I-I-I think he might have just wanted to scare the shit out of me. And he d-d-did a really good j-j-job."

I realize then that her teeth have started chattering, not from cold. From shock. With a hiss, I unclasp and peel off her bra, then her panties. Then I peel off my own sopping clothes. Naked, I draw her against me, wanting only to hold her, to keep her safe, to protect her from the whole fucking world.

We stand under the pounding water, my arms around her until she stops shaking, her teeth stop chattering. Then I turn off the shower, wrap her in a towel and carry her to the bed. I climb in beside her and pulling her tight against me.

"What the fuck am I supposed to do with you?" I ask.

"Make love to me," she says, those gorgeous blue eyes finding mine. "Make love to me so I stop thinking about how you could have been shot. Killed. How I could have lost you. How—"

I rest my fingertip against her lush lips.

"I told you to play dead. To stay safe."

"You didn't exactly tell me," she says. "It was more of a slight head shake that I had to interpret—"

My lips crash down on hers. She tastes like salt, like sea water.

She wraps her arms around me, one hand tangling in my wet hair, the other clasping my shoulder. Her moan vibrates through her, through me as I roll atop her.

I lick the seam of her lips, demanding she open to me, pushing inside. I cup the back of her head, kissing her, tasting her, taking what I want. I want her. All of her. Every part of her is mine.

Cupping her breast, I skim the pad of my thumb

over her nipple. She gasps and arches into my touch. I kiss her neck, her collarbone, the swell of her breast. Then I close my lips around her taut nipple, sucking on the sensitive peak. I move back and forth, kissing her breasts, sucking and licking her nipples, her sighs and gasps making me rock hard.

I slide my hand between her thighs and find the slick folds of her pussy. "Such a good girl. So wet," I murmur, pushing my finger inside her.

She wriggles and sighs as I push a second finger into her wet heat. I grind the heel of my palm against her clit while I work my fingers in and out, making her whimper. Her hips shift restlessly beneath me. My cock is so hard it hurts.

This girl. This fucking gorgeous, brave girl.

I want to make this slow, to draw out her moans and sighs and cries, to make her shake and beg, to see her drenched in sweat, her thighs slick with her arousal. So I take my time, stroking her, teasing her.

"Damian." My name is a plea. "Damian, please. Oh, god, that feels so good." She arches into me and presses her lips to mine. "I need you inside me. I want to come with you inside me."

I don't make her repeat herself. I push her thighs apart and shift atop her, lacing our fingers together. "Look at me," I order, and she does, her eyes on mine, pupils dark and dilated with arousal.

I push the head of my cock inside her, pull back, push forward, going deeper with each thrust until I'm all the way in, her sweet pussy so tight, so hot. "Fucking gorgeous," I say as I move, watching her expression as she arches her body, taking all of me, her eyes never leaving mine.

Her breathing is ragged and shallow as she matches

my rhythm, her hips working in tandem with mine. Perfect synchrony.

I feel my orgasm building, twisting tighter and tighter, but only when she screams my name, her whole body shuddering do I let myself go, let myself come in a hurricane of sensation, my body, my thoughts consumed by her. Consumed by this woman who sacrificed her freedom for her brother, who shot a man to keep me safe, who braved an ocean to save me from loss and grief. This woman who was neither born into my world nor raised in it, but who adapts and bends and survives. This woman who is like no other.

Alina Madsen is mine. She will always be mine.

She just doesn't know it yet.

26

Alina

"I NEED TO TELL YOU SOMETHING," I whisper as I lie wrapped in Damian's arms. He believed in me, fought his brother for me. I want to tell him what I know. "I didn't tell you in the beginning because I was saving it as my trump card. I thought I could use it to save Markus or to buy him more time or something."

"Your trump card?" he asks, and I feel his lips against the top of my head.

It would be easier to tell him like this, wrapped in his arms, not having to see the disappointment and betrayal in his eyes. But I'm not a coward. So I sit up and look down at him. He's lying on his back, one arm under his head, the sheets down around his hips, his perfect, chiseled torso bare.

"Keep looking at me like that and the only words coming out of your mouth will be my name and 'please'," he says.

I shake my head and rest my hand on his chest. I feel the steady beat of his heart.

"I should have said something sooner. At first, I

didn't tell you because I didn't trust you. I didn't tell you because information is power, and this information was the only power I had. When Leo was questioning me, I didn't tell him because he would have thought I kept it secret because I was a spy. But I need to tell you now…"

His dark eyes study me, his expression unreadable.

I wet my lips. "Enzo never talked to me about work. But I overheard one-sided conversations more than once. He spoke to the Ivanovs. He did jobs for them. One night when we were at La Vecchia, Mikhail Ivanov was there. I didn't know who he was. Enzo didn't introduce me. But I saw a picture in the paper and I figured it out. They talked for a long time. Mikhail gave him an envelope that I'm pretty sure was stuffed with cash."

Damian's quiet for a long moment. My heart pounds. I feel sick.

Then he says, "Bianchi works for the Ivanovs."

It isn't a question, but I answer anyway. "I think so, yeah."

Damian runs his fingers through my hair, staring at the strands as they slide off his palm. Then he raises his gaze to mine. "You didn't tell me because you thought it was information you could trade at a later date. Maybe save your brother's ass. Or save your own."

"Yes," I whisper. "I was saving it for the right time."

He nods. "I would have done the same. It was a good strategy. So why tell me now?"

"Because it's information you need to find the man who killed your father. I don't know if it was Enzo, but even if it wasn't, he's involved somehow. It's information you need and I want you to have it."

He smiles, a flash of white teeth against tan skin and dark three-day stubble. I don't think a more beautiful man has ever existed.

"Thank you," he says, and pulls me down into the cradle of his arms, holding me against his heart.

I HEAR THE STATEROOM DOOR CLOSE WHEN DAMIAN SLIPS out. He thought I was asleep. I wasn't. I watched him as he pulled on worn jeans and a t-shirt. I watched him as he took Leo's knife from the table and left the room.

I pull on shorts and a tank top and follow.

He heads for the swim deck. The blond gunman I shot is there, wrists and ankles bound, then looped together and pulled behind his back. Hog-tied. He's lying on his side in a pool of his own blood. His face is bruised and battered. Three of Leo's men guard him, guns drawn.

I stand on the deck above, watching as Damian kicks the blond gunman over onto his back. The guy groans as the movement jerks his injured shoulder.

I'm the one who put that hole in him. I should feel terrible. I don't.

Damian hunkers down beside him, grabs his hair and jerks the guy's head back. He stares at him a moment then releases him, glances over his shoulder and asks, "He tell you anything?"

Whoever he's speaking to is out of my line of sight.

"He and the others are mercenaries." It's Leo's voice. "Hired by Nicole. He was kind enough to share the names of his associates. I have reached out to our people and confirmed his claim. They are known mercenaries." Leonardo limps into view. He's wearing the clothes he had on earlier, rumpled and creased and still a little damp. His right pant leg has been cut off mid-thigh, his leg wrapped in a white bandage. He lifts his hands and laces his fingers together behind his neck, then arches in a stretch. His knuckles are red and bloody.

"What's his association with the Ivanovs?" Damian asks.

"There isn't one. Nicole hired him and his associates to kill me. Revenge for her father."

"Did you kill her father?" Damian asks. "She said it was a bomb. Never known you to kill from a distance when you can do it up close and personal."

I shiver, remembering how up close and personal Leo was with me just this morning.

"I didn't kill her father. I've never planted a bomb in my life," Leo says. "But I'm going to find out who did. And I'm going to find out why they want her to believe it was me."

"Is he of any further use?" Damian asks with a gesture at the bound mercenary.

"No," Leo says.

Damian nods, grabs the man by the hair, yanks his head back and slits his throat using the knife he took from the stateroom. Blood spurts out, soaking the man's clothes and the deck beneath him. The wound at his throat gapes.

I press my hand to my mouth and stumble back a step.

Straightening, Damian turns and looks right at me, his expression set in stone, his eyes dark and fathomless.

This is who I am. This is what I am.

He knew I wasn't sleeping. He knew I would follow him. And he knew all along I was standing here, watching. He wanted me to see this, to see *him*, no rose-colored glasses, no fairy-tale misconceptions. I told him the truth. This is his way of doing the same.

I wrap my arms around myself and watch as he shoves the corpse into the waves.

He stares down at the blood-stained deck for a second, shakes his head and looks at Leo. "Bastard stained the fucking teak," he says. "We're going to have to replace it."

I turn and go back to the stateroom. Damian doesn't join me. Not then and not later.

When we dock, it's Luca who comes to get me, who brings me to shore, who accompanies me in the helicopter. It's Luca who stares out the window while I cry, the horror and confusion of the day overwhelming me. Luca who finally takes my hand in his and holds it until we land at Harrah's. Luca who drives me back to the condo.

Luca who gives me a phone. Not the ancient phone Damian took from me. A new one with the same number and my contacts transferred. Not that I have many of those.

There's a number on it that I didn't have before. Damian's.

"Leo will be coming by to speak with you tomorrow," Luca says. "Get some rest." Then he places a key card on the kitchen island. The key card for the elevator.

I unpack after he leaves, tossing the pink dress in the trash. I never want to see it again, never mind wear it.

After a shower, I crawl into bed. Leo will be coming to speak with me tomorrow… Alone? I have no clue. Just like I have no clue what he plans to say. Will Damian be with him? Do I want him to be?

He showed me who he is, who he really is. I knew it all along, but seeing it, seeing him kill a bound man and push the body into the waves…

Why do I miss him? Why do I wish he was here with

me right now? Why do I crave his presence, the sound of his voice, the feel of his arms around me?

Because he is exactly what I thought him to be the very first time I saw him: a demon-angel. A monster. A man who loves his family. A killer. A man capable of both good and evil. A man I'm falling in love with. What does that say about me?

Wrapping my arms around myself, I fight the tears that prick my lids.

I feel so confused. So alone.

I stare at my phone. Then I call Markus. It goes to voicemail.

Guess I really didn't expect anything else.

Leo arrives at the condo the following morning. He knocks. I didn't expect that.

"May I come in?" he asks when I answer the door. I didn't expect that either.

His lip is split, his jaw bruised. I glance at his hands. The knuckles are red and raw. Remnants of his fight with Damian yesterday. Or maybe remnants of his interrogation of the mercenary.

"Sure. Come on in." I pull the door wide and step to the side so he can walk past me. I peer into the foyer. There's no one else there. Not Luca, not Joe, not Vito.

Not Damian.

I swallow and close the door, then turn to face Leo, oddly unafraid. I've realized that what I told Damian yesterday is true. If Leonardo Russo wanted me dead, I'd be dead. He just wanted to scare the shit out of me. Which he did, very efficiently. But he's here today for a different reason. I just don't know what it is, yet.

"You, um, want coffee?" I ask.

"Coffee?" His brows rise.

I shrug. "I'm a little uncertain of the etiquette here. You know, how one is supposed to act when one is visited by a man who recently had his hand wrapped around one's throat, strangling one."

"Ah." He gestures toward the sectional. "Shall we?"

I perch on the edge as he settles back comfortably, one arm stretched along the back of the sofa, legs spread.

"I owe you an apology," he says. One more thing I did not expect.

"Go ahead," I say.

He tips his head looking confused.

"Go ahead and apologize," I say. "You said you owe me an apology but you actually didn't offer one."

One side of his mouth curves a little. "I apologize," he says.

"For what?" I ask. "I prefer specifics. Is it just a general 'sorry for being an asshole' or a specific 'sorry for almost murdering you' or does it include 'sorry for accusing you of being a spy.'" When he says nothing for a long moment, I say, "Have you actually ever apologized to anyone before?"

"Not recently." He picks an imaginary bit of lint off his sleeve.

"Just dive in," I suggest. "It'll hurt less."

He ignores that and says. "What do you want?"

"Want? I don't understand."

"I wronged you on several levels. I owe you for that. You shot a man to save my brother. I owe you for that. You dove into the ocean to try to save me. I owe you for that. You provided my brother with valuable information about Bianchi. I owe you for that. I am not in the habit of owing anything to anyone. So what do you want?"

I don't even need to think about it. "Forgive my brother's debt."

Leo studies me for a moment. "That's all? Forgive a million dollar debt?"

I can't tell if he finds the request acceptable or outlandish. So I say nothing. I just wait for him to speak again.

"You want nothing for yourself?" he asks, his dark eyes locked on mine as he leans forward so his elbows rest on his splayed knees.

Why do I feel like this is a trap?

"I want you to forgive my brother's debt." I pause. "And the interest."

He laughs, his whole face relaxing, making him look younger, less terrifying. "Smart girl."

"So that's it? No more debt?"

He nods and rises. "Done. No more debt." Then he walks toward the door, leaving me sitting on the couch with my heart pounding and my palms damp.

"Wait," I say. He glances back at me, his expression unreadable. "What about Damian?"

"What about him?"

Markus's debt is forgiven. What does that mean for me? Am I still Damian's prisoner? I don't know what to say, how to ask.

Maybe I imagine it, but for a second, I think Leo's expression softens just a little.

"I suggest you ask him," he says, then walks through the door, closing it firmly behind him.

27

Alina

FOR THREE DAYS, I sit in the condo, waiting for Damian to come. He never does.

Luca, Vito, and Joe are nowhere to be seen. I'm completely alone.

I call Markus constantly, but he never answers. I leave dozens of voicemails which he doesn't return. Leo said the debt is forgiven, but my dumbass brother could have already gotten himself into a brand new mess with a whole different group of shady people. It's kind of his modus operandi.

I think about Damian all the time. I dream about him, fantasize about him, ache for his touch and his smile and the way he looks at me like I am the most beautiful woman he's ever seen. I miss the sound of his voice and the sound of his laughter. I miss the way he listens when I speak and cares about my opinions.

I almost call him a thousand times, but I don't know what to say. *Hey, I know you're a criminal, and I'm okay with that. I know you have few scruples, and I'm okay with that. I watched you kill a man and I know you've killed men before and will kill more men in the future, and I'm okay with that.*

Am I, though?

That's the question. And I don't have an answer.

Finally, on the fourth morning, I call him.

He doesn't answer, but twenty minutes later, he walks in through the front door.

He looks good. Better than good. Despite the bruise on his cheek and the healing split lip, souvenirs from his fight with his brother, he is the most beautiful thing I've ever seen. Black suit. White shirt. No tie. The top two buttons of his shirt undone to reveal a V of naked skin and a hint of his tattoos. A platinum watch on his wrist and a ring on his left index finger. A man who knows how to accessorize.

"Asshole," I say as he comes to stand in front of me. I'm so glad he's here. I'm so angry he hasn't reached out to me for three days. I don't know where I stand. Where *we* stand. Where I *want* to stand.

"I brought croissants," he says, holding out a bag.

I take it from him and ask, "Chocolate?"

"What else?" he asks with a lift of one dark brow.

With a strangled sob, I punch him in the arm.

He cocks his head, studying me more closely. "You're pissed at me."

"Furious."

"Why the hell are you furious?"

I pace to the kitchen and set the bag of croissants on the island. Then I turn to face him. "Because."

Damian hisses out a breath of frustration. "Because why?"

Because I didn't know where you were. If you were okay. If you were safe. If I can accept the reality of who and what you are.

If you were coming back to me. If you still want me. If I have a place in your life now that my brother's debt is forgiven.

Because I don't know if you feel for me even a tiny bit of what I feel for you.

I can't say any of that. Not yet. I'm not ready. Instead, I say, "Because I didn't hear from you." I cringe as I say it. I sound pathetic and needy.

"I was giving you time to process the…events on the boat. To decide…"

We stare at each other in silence.

There are a million things I want to say to him. A million things I'm afraid to say.

Finally, I blurt, "I can't reach my brother. I've called Markus a million times. He isn't answering. I left him at least a dozen messages to call me back, to let me know he's okay. But there's nothing. No reply, no messages. He could be dead."

"He's not dead."

I blink. "You know where he is, don't you? Where is he? Is he okay?"

"He's fine," he tells me. "Just leave it alone, Alina."

"Not a chance. I need to talk to him." I shake my head. "If you know where he is, why won't you tell me?"

"Leave it alone," he growls, and the cold flat tone makes my heart skip a beat. Something in my expression makes him hiss out another frustrated breath. "He doesn't want you to know where he is. I gave him my word."

I feel like I've been slapped. My brother doesn't want me to know where he is. That can only mean something terrible. But Damian's implacable expression tells me I won't get any more information out of him.

"So what now?" I whisper. "I go back to my apartment and my job at the Emerald? I go back to my life?"

His jaw tenses. "You no longer have an apartment or a job, but, yes, you go back to your life."

I stare at him, feeling the floor drop out from under me. "This is goodbye?"

His dark gaze bores into me. "If that's what you want."

"What I want?" I yell. "What I want is for you to talk to me, to tell me—" I break off, my anger and pain and despair making it impossible to speak. He made me care about him. Made me lov—

I force my emotions under control and ask, "What do *you* want, Damian?"

He rakes his fingers back through his dark hair, leaving it disheveled and sexy, making me want to run my fingers through it, to pull his head down and press my mouth to his.

"Don't look at me like that, Alina," he says, his voice low and rough. "For the first time in my fucking life, I'm trying to do the honorable thing."

"The honorable thing. You say it like it's a foreign concept for you. But it isn't," I say, moving to stand directly in front of him, close enough that I can smell the scent of his skin, citrus and spice. "You did the honorable thing when you defended me from Leo on the boat. I don't know all the ins and outs of crime syndicates, but I suspect that going against the boss is a big deal. You did the honorable thing when you lied to Nicole and the mercenaries to protect me, when you told them I was asleep in the stateroom. You did the honorable thing when you threw yourself on your father to try to save his life. I think that this isn't the first time in your life that you're doing the honorable thing. I think you always do the honorable thing. It's just that your code of honor is very different than the one that holds sway in the world I know."

He looks down at his hands, at the bruised and split knuckles. "You know my hands aren't clean," he says. "They're dirty. Filthy, actually. And I'm okay with that. I don't have any plans to choose a different path. The business...my family business...it's my life. And it's violent and dirty and dangerous as fuck. And it's everything I live and breathe to protect."

"I understand," I tell him.

"No. An outsider could never understand. Not really. The business isn't what you see on the surface—the headlines or the rumors. It's about pride, about blood, about dirt and grease and the very fiber of life itself. We live outside of the rules because the rules were meant for normal people. We're not normal and we don't want to be."

He's telling me I have to choose. Him, or everything I've believed my whole life. Good and bad. Right and wrong. Laws. Rules. Everything I've been taught about civilization.

He's right. I'm an outsider. The question is, do I want to stay an outsider or do I want to become part of his world?

28

Damian

Alina watched me kill a man. I gave her time to come to terms with that.

But maybe I shouldn't have. Maybe I should have left the yacht with her, stuck to her side like a burr, forced her to accept me and my world.

Or maybe I should have stayed away longer, let her miss me, ache for me, let her yearning guide her decision.

She rests her palm on my cheek, those gorgeous blue eyes locked on mine.

I want to demand an answer, demand she reveal all her thoughts and dreams, demand that she give every part of herself to me.

Instead, I catch her hand and press a kiss to the center of her palm. All the demands in the world will not make her stay. This, she must choose. Because the choice is not just me, but my way of life, my world, my family. And once she's in, she's in for life. No way out. No going back.

If I were anything but a selfish bastard, I would let

her go. Hell, I'd fucking chase her off.

But I *am* a selfish bastard. So I will make her want me, need me, ache for me. I will make her trust me. Make her love me. I want every part of her—her love, her loyalty, her body, her soul.

Because, yeah, I fucking love Alina Madsen. I'm so fucking in love with her I don't know which way is up.

I loop my arm around her waist and pull her against me, her body pliant, willing. I lower my head and kiss her, taking my time, tasting her, teasing her.

I don't let myself consider that this might be the last time I kiss her, touch her, take her. I only let myself think of this moment.

I lick her lips, push my tongue into her mouth then withdraw. A lure. A dance.

With a soft moan, she comes up on her toes, molds herself against me, her breasts pressed to my chest. Her fingers lace through my hair, pulling me closer. Without breaking the kiss, I shrug out of my suit jacket, letting it lie where it falls. She's panting as I walk her backward to the bedroom and tumble us both onto the bed, catching my weight on my forearms.

She reaches for the buttons of my shirt, undoing them one by one, pressing soft kisses to my skin, her lips warm. Then she reaches for my belt, sliding it free.

I flip us both so she is atop me, and slowly strip her clothes from her body, taking my time, sliding each garment off as I kiss and lick and nip her perfect pale skin. Her naked breasts tempt me and I shift us until I sit at the edge of the bed with Alina straddling me. Then I take her pebbled nipple in my mouth, licking and sucking.

She exhales a shuddering breath. I slide my fingers between her legs and stroke her wet pussy, her clit, making her sigh and pump her hips. Sweat slicks her skin. Her soft, panting breaths reach inside me and twists my lust to a razor's edge.

Reaching down between her legs, she layers her fingers next to mine, gathering her own moisture. Then she closes her slick hand around my cock, stroking, pumping, and finally, positioning me at her opening.

She sinks down on me slowly, her eyes locked on mine, her pupils dark and dilated.

"Fuck," I say on a rough exhale. I want to roll atop her and sink deep and fuck her till she screams. My muscles twitch with the effort of holding back, of letting her play, letting her take control.

She puts both hands on my shoulders, pushing me down so I lie on my back, and she rides me, head thrown back. Her tempo picks up. I curl my fingers into her thighs, my hips pumping of their own accord.

"Your pussy is so tight, so fucking perfect," I say.

I feel my orgasm building in my balls, my thighs, the small of my back.

"Oh, God, Damian." She moans, gasps, her hips moving in time with mine, our bodies poised on the edge of a cliff.

She screams as she comes and collapses atop me as my I tumble into my own release, my whole body shuddering with pleasure.

I gather her against me, my chin resting on the top of her head as I pull the bedsheets over us.

There are words that hover at the tip of my tongue. Words that will bind her to me. I know they will. And so, I don't say them aloud. It goes against my nature, my inclination, my wants and desires, but I will wait for her to choose.

Fuck me, but I love her enough to let her choose.

29

Alina

Something pulls me out of a deep dreamless sleep. I'm alone in the bed. Damian got a call and left a couple of hours ago. One more thing I need to consider. He is a Mafia prince. He'll always answer the summons, no matter when it comes. Can I live with that?

Can I live with everything he is and everything he isn't?

I close my eyes, fighting the lump in my throat.

The more honest questions is: Can I live without him? Can I see my future without him in it?

I imagine my life in the months, years, decades to come. And the only life I want is one with Damian in it.

A buzzing sensation comes from beneath my pillow. That must be what woke me. I fumble for the phone and glance at the screen.

I need to see you. URGENT.

A breath catches in my chest. Markus.

I call my brother. He doesn't answer.

Where are you? Why aren't you answering?

Can't answer right now. Meet me. EMERGENCY.

I stare at the screen, my pulse pounding. Leo told me my brother's debt is forgiven. But just because he no longer owes money to the Russos doesn't mean Markus hasn't gone and gotten himself into another mess. That's his pattern. Has been for a very long time. Drink too much. Fall in with a shitty crowd. Use drugs. Gamble. Lose a lot of money. Rinse. Repeat.

I almost tell him I'm not coming, that he's on his own. Almost.

Then I sigh.

What's the emergency?

He's going to kill me.

My heart stutters in my chest.

Who? Who's going to kill you?
Markus? Answer me.
Markus?!

He doesn't answer. I stare at the phone, willing a text to come through, worry and fear swirling through me. Who's going to kill him? Leo said his debt is forgiven. Damian... He wouldn't hurt my brother. Not now. Not after everything.

Whoever is after my brother, it isn't the Russos.

I wait, minutes feeling like hours. When Markus doesn't answer, I text.

I'll meet you. Where?

Come alone. Don't tell anyone.

He sends me the address.

The Emerald. Not sure why he wants to meet there, but I'm not about to waste time asking.

I pull on jeans and a t-shirt then I call a ride.

The Emerald isn't in a good neighborhood. It isn't surrounded by shiny new casinos, luxury stores, and tourist traps. The ugly, squat, concrete building sits between an auto supply place and a half-vacant strip mall. There's an electrical wholesaler across the street. The Emerald's bright red sign boasts a black silhouette of a naked girl with the words Gentlemen's Club Open 24 Hours in stark white. This place is for those who can't afford five-star entertainment. But it serves strong drinks and cheap food. And the girls who dance on the stage, wrapping themselves acrobatically and erotically around the poles, work damn hard for the money.

The street is empty when I climb out of the car. The second I close the door, the driver takes off, leaving me standing under a burned-out street lamp. Markus said he'd be waiting outside, but I don't see anyone. I check to see if he's texted again.

Nothing.

So I text him.

No reply.

I'm just about to head inside when a shadow detaches from a the doorway of the auto supply. My brother stands in the shadows, shoulders hunched, his hands in the pockets of his oversized black sweatshirt, the hood pulled up.

I raise a hand in greeting, dropping it after a second when he doesn't wave back.

The fine hairs at my nape prickle and rise. And in that second, I know I've made a terrible mistake.

Too late. He's already walking toward me with that familiar swagger.

Ice rushes through my veins.

Keeping my hands behind my back, I reach into my purse and pull out my phone. I hope the darkness and the shadows hide my actions as I risk a quick glance and hit dial. It goes to voicemail. I don't disconnect, just shove my phone into the back pocket of my jeans.

"Alina."

I freeze at the sound of Enzo's far-too-familiar voice, like the chilling rasp of a phantom I'd thought was dead and buried. He's right in front of me now.

"Where's Markus?" I manage, the words dry and choked.

"You were always a little too worried about that brother of yours. I see that hasn't changed." His voice sounds smug, like it pleases him to see me distressed.

"Why do you have his phone, Enzo? What have you done to him?"

"Me?" He affects an innocent expression. "Maybe you should ask the guy you're *fucking*. Ask him why your brother's disappeared, leaving his truck, his clothes, even his phone behind. I have his phone because I visited his place, looking for you. His phone was just sitting there on his dresser, begging to be taken. Figured if there was one way to get you to meet me, it was by pretending to be your worthless brother."

I take a step back, my heart pounding, my thoughts spinning. I think of Damian telling me not to ask questions about Markus' whereabouts, telling me my brother doesn't want me to know where he is.

I think about the debt Markus owed, a million dollars, and Leo agreeing to erase it. Maybe he meant it was erased because Markus is dead.

No. Damian wouldn't do that to me. I know he wouldn't.

"Why did you want to meet here, at the Emerald?" I ask, my voice loud, hopefully loud enough that Damian's voicemail picks it up.

"Nostalgia. I watched you, you know. I can't tell you how many times I watched you leave work. So close. But I couldn't touch you. Couldn't go near you. That fucker was looking for me. He had a tail on you, waiting for me to show."

Enzo steps even closer and grabs my arm, yanking me along as he starts walking. Then he pulls my purse from my grasp and throws it in a Dumpster as we pass.

"You won't be needing that," he says. "You won't be needing money or your phone. I've got you, Alina." He picks up speed, dragging me along. I look around, frantic, but the street's deserted.

"I want to kill him," he says as he drags me off the main street toward a deserted warehouse. "For even thinking he can touch you. He took you to get to me. Fucker. Bastard. I'll kill him. I'll fucking kill him like I killed his fucking father."

I gasp. "You killed Salvatore Russo."

Enzo just yanks my arm harder. His grip is bruising. His pace so fast, I stumble. He hauls me upright and keeps going.

"Where are you taking me?" I ask, digging in my heels and trying to drag him to a stop.

He wasn't expecting that. His grip on my arm eases just a little.

I lift my knee as if intending to get him in the nuts, then slam my forearm as hard as I can across his throat instead. For a split second, his grip loosens. I pull away and run back toward the Emerald, screaming at the top of my lungs.

"Bitch. You fucking bitch!" Enzo snarls from behind me.

I hear his feet on the pavement, gaining on me.

Heart slamming against my ribs, I tear across the parking lot, chest heaving, legs pumping.

If I can just make it to the Emerald…

Suddenly, a dark sedan pulls directly in my path, tires squealing, cutting off my escape.

30

Alina

A SECOND DARK sedan pulls in behind the first. The doors fly open. Four men step out, all dressed in black.

In the split second before I recognize them, my terror expands and swallows me whole. Then Damian holds out his arm and I run to him, throwing myself against him. He pulls me in to his side, his arm a band of steel around me.

"Did he hurt you?" he asks, his voice deadly calm. Despite that, I can feel the rage pounding through him.

"No," I whisper.

He looks down, catches my chin and tilts my head so he can look into my eyes. His expression is flat, cold, his demon-angel eyes burning. "Did he hurt you?" he asks again.

"He yanked my arm. Dragged me away from the club."

He nods, then glances over to where Luca has Enzo pinned on the ground. He walks over and stands over Enzo, then puts his foot on Enzo's wrist pinning it to the ground. He takes his gun from his waist and slowly screws on a silencer, taking his time while Enzo struggles and spits curses.

"You laid hands on her," Damian says, his voice like ice. "Grabbed her, you fucking worthless piece of shit. You bruised her. Hit her." He leans down and places the silencer against the back of Enzo's hand where all the tendons cross the wrist.

He fires point blank.

Enzo howls and jerks against Luka's hold.

I wrap my arms around myself and stumble back, sagging against the side of the car. From this distance, in the darkness, I can't see the blood and bits of shattered bone, but I know they're there.

Damian glances at me, then at Joe. "Alina might be more comfortable in the car," he says. "Put the music on. Something loud."

"No," I say, straightening of the side of the car. I'm not going to hide. I'm not going to pretend that I don't know what Damian does, who he is. What he is.

He holds my gaze for a long moment, then gives a short nod. Turning away, he shifts his stance, squatting down so he's eye level with Enzo.

"You killed my father," he says. "Thank you for the admission of guilt, by the way. That was easy."

"I admitted nothing," Enzo snarls.

"But you did," Damian says. He pulls out his phone and plays back his voicemail, which cuts out right after Enzo admits to killing Damian's father.

"You bitch," Enzo howls, struggling against Luca's hold, his face contorting with hate and rage and fear as he tries to lunge for me. "You fucking bitch."

Damian backhands Enzo hard enough to send his head snapping back. "Watch your mouth," he says.

He rises and presses the sole of his shoe down on Enzo's other wrist.

"Wait," Enzo says, struggling, trying to pull free. "You don't need to do this. Wait."

Damian laughs, the sound chilling. "You don't get to tell me what I do and don't need to do, Bianchi. But I'll tell you what, though. Answer my question, just one question, and this all stops."

"What question?"

"Who paid you?"

"I can't," Enzo says, shaking his head. "They'll kill me."

This time, it's Luca who laughs, sounding genuinely amused.

"And you think Damian won't kill you?" he asks.

Enzo shoots a desperate look at me. "Alina—"

Damian presses the silencer down hard on Enzo's wrist and shoots.

Enzo howls and sobs.

"You don't say her name," Damian says. "You don't look at her. You are not fit to even breathe the same air as her." He grabs Enzo's hair again and jerks his head up. "Last chance, Bianchi. You tell me who paid you and this ends. Or you stay silent and I take you to my brother. Leo enjoys a good question and answer period. He'll cut off parts of you, take his time, peel your skin off in strips. He'll make it last, even after you give up every secret you've ever known."

When Enzo says nothing, Damian shrugs and steps away. "Leo will be very happy to see you."

"No!" Enzo howls. "Please. It was Mikhail."

"Mikhail who?" Damian says softly. "Full name. Who hired you to kill my father?"

Enzo's sobbing now, tears and snot running down his face. "Mikhail Ivanov."

"Thank you," Damian says.

Luca lets go of Enzo, rises and steps away.

Enzo stays on the ground, hunched over his ruined hands, sobbing.

"I'm a man of my word," Damian says. "This all stops."

Enzo looks up. "Thank you. Thank you—"

Damian shoots him through the head and the heart.

I sink back against the car, feeling numb. He killed Enzo. Killed him the same way that Enzo killed Damian's father. Killed him just like I've dreamed of killing the man who killed my parents.

"Bring him," Damian says to Luca, striding toward me. He rests his butt against the car beside me and slouches down. We're side by side, our shoulders touching.

Luca grabs Enzo's feet while Joe hooks him under the arms. They carry his body over to the first sedan and shove him into the trunk. Vito slams it shut. Then the three men get into the car and drive away, leaving Damian and me alone.

He takes my hand and leads me around to the passenger side of the sedan, opens the door and waits as I get in. Then he rounds the hood and climbs in.

"My purse is in the Dumpster," I say.

He shoots me a look, his dark eyes flat and cold. With a sigh, he gets out. I wait in the dark until he returns, purse in hand.

"Your phone?" he says.

"In my back pocket."

Wordlessly, he holds out his hand. I pull out my phone and unlock it. Pulling up the text exchange between me and Enzo, who I thought was Markus, I hand him the phone so he can read it. He doesn't. He just holds my phone, his gaze locked on mine.

"You thought you were meeting your brother?"

I nod.

"You know that saying about doing the same thing again and again and expecting a different result?" he says. "You snuck out of our bed to talk to your brother for the second time. The first time, you pissed me off. This time, you could have been killed."

His tone is flat, too flat, like he's forcing every bit of emotion from his words, his thoughts because allowing even a tiny speck to leak through will open a floodgate he can't stop.

"But you got Enzo, and you got a name," I reason. "That's what you wanted, right?"

He sighs. He doesn't read the text exchange. Instead, he adds contacts to my phone.

"What are you doing?" I ask.

"Adding Luca, Joe, and Vito's numbers." He hands me back the phone without reading the text exchange.

He's telling me in the clearest way possible that he trusts me, that he knows I didn't sneak out to meet Enzo, that he knows I'm telling the truth.

I press my lips together and fight the tears that threaten to fall.

"You okay?" he asks.

I swallow. "Not exactly."

With a nod, he pulls into the street. His hands are relaxed on the wheel, but I can feel the vibrating tension coming off him in waves.

He doesn't talk, just drives, and after a few minutes, I realize we're in an unfamiliar part of Vegas. We pull up in front of a low rise building with views of the Las

Vegas skyline and the mountains. The building itself is beautiful, pale stucco and warm wood.

"Where are we?" I ask.

"Home," Damian says. His tone doesn't invite more questions, so I tag along as he unlocks a door, leads me inside and flicks on the lights.

My breath catches. If the condo I've been staying in is gorgeous, this place is sublime. I turn a full circle. The kitchen is beautiful with a waterfall island and a million cabinets. The dining room and adjoining living room lead out to a massive terrace with outdoor seating and a dining table and even a barbecue. And everywhere I look I see Damian's stamp. Elegant with just a hint of glitz.

Home. He said we were going home. Not to the soulless condo that lacked anything personal.

To his home. His real home.

I spin and stare at him, my heart ponding.

His gaze searches my face, then he pulls me into his embrace. I wrap my arms around his waist, my cheek to his chest, his heartbeat steady and reassuring.

"Do you know where my brother is? Do you know if he's okay?" I ask.

I feel his sigh.

"He asked me not to tell you, just in case he fails."

That makes no sense. "Fails?" When Damian makes no reply, I say, "You gave Markus your word that you wouldn't tell me?"

"Yeah."

"Did you give him your word that you wouldn't confirm it if I guess right?"

He's quiet for a second. "No."

"Is he in rehab? He didn't want you to tell me in case he doesn't get clean? In case he fails?"

Again, he's quiet, then he says, "Yes."

Tears sting my eyes. Markus is in rehab.

"Are you paying for his rehab?" I ask.

"Yes."

I tighten my arms around his waist. Markus is safe. Better than safe. He's working on getting well. And Damian is making that happen.

"Why are you doing this for him?" I ask.

He smiles, his real smile, the one that creates the tiny crinkles at the corners of his eyes. "I'm doing it for you." He runs the backs of his fingers along my cheek.

For me. I don't know what to do with that, how to process my emotions.

"How did you get to me so fast?" I ask, thinking that it had only been a few minutes between the time I left him the voicemail and the time he showed up with Luca and Vito and Joe.

"Tracker on your phone," Damian says. "But that was smart, leaving me the message so I could find you."

"A tracker on my…" I should be angry. He put a tracker on my phone without my knowledge or consent. But if he hadn't, Enzo could have taken me who knows where.

"I have enemies that will use you to get to me, Alina. I need to know where you are. Always," he says. "Need to know where to find you. Sabina has trackers in her earrings and the ring she always wears, just in case they take her phone."

They. He's talking about enemies. About the Ivanovs or any other group who would take Sabina as a hostage to use against the Russos. Take *me* as a hostage.

"How could anyone use me to get to you?" I ask. I know. In my heart, I know. But I want, *need* to hear the words.

He lowers his head and rests his forehead against

mine. "I didn't plan this, Alina. Didn't plan to want you. Need you. I never planned to make myself weak."

"Damian—"

He cuts me off with a finger against my lips. "You are a liability. A way to get to me. And I don't fucking care. You are worth more to me than my own fucking life. Do you understand what I'm saying?"

"I…" I stare up at him, at the hard line of his jaw and his unsmiling mouth, at his dark, fathomless eyes, and I say, "I love you, Damian. I love you so much."

He cups my cheeks, his gaze locked on mine. His expression is hard, intent. "If you choose me, Alina, it's forever. You get that, right?"

My heart swells. "Yes," I whisper. "I get that." Then I smile. "If you choose me, Damian, it's forever."

"I chose you the night we met. Love at fucking first sight." His voice is rough, like the words are torn from somewhere deep inside.

"You sure that wasn't just lust?" I ask.

"Lust, yeah." He runs the pad of his thumb against my lower lip. "But it's more than that. I love that you're strong. Brave. Smart. Funny. I love the sounds you make when you come. I love the parts of your soul that you shared with the world when you wrote your short story. I love the way you tilt your head when you have a question. I love the way you hold it together when shit gets rough. I love your loyalty. I fucking love you, Alina Madsen."

"I fucking love you, too, Damian Russo."

He lowers his head and kisses me, his lips on mine, possessive, like he's imprinting himself on my soul with that kiss.

"I need to go. Leo will be expecting me," he says. "I'm having someone pack up your belongings and bring them here. Give yourself a tour. Bedroom's upstairs to the right. Upstairs to the left is your writing room."

"My—"

"Desk. Laptop. Bookshelves…" He reaches into his breast pocket and pulls out an Amex Black card. He hands it to me. "Anything I didn't think of, just order."

I stare at him, hope and joy and a little trepidation mixing in my veins. "Are you asking me to move in with you?" I whisper.

"Not asking," he says.

"So let me get this straight," I say. "I'm a liability. A weakness. You are not asking but rather telling me I'm moving in…"

He waits for me to continue.

I don't.

Damian nods slowly. "You've seen who I am. What I do. I understand your hesitation."

"My only hesitation is the fact that you're bossy as fuck." I swallow, thinking of what he told me about his dad. "What if I give you my entire heart, my life, my everything, and you see some other blonde who catches your eye?"

His lips quirk. "No other blondes. Maybe a brunette…"

When I narrow my eyes, he laughs, that gorgeous, warm, happy laugh.

"I don't want anyone else. You're it for me, Alina Madsen. Only you. Got it? I told you the night you agreed to become my captive, I don't cheat."

I search his face, but see no deception. Only sincerity.

"Be with me, Alina. Here. Everywhere. Forever."

Again, he waits for a reply.

It doesn't take long before he gets one this time. "Okay."

He raises a brow. "Okay what?"

"I'll be with you, Damian. Here. Everywhere. Forever." A smile tugs at my lips. "Asshole."

"Good." Then he pulls me against him for a hard, swift kiss.

I've fallen madly in love with Damian Russo—mafia prince, killer, criminal. And Damian Russo loves me too. I watch as he walks out the door, knowing he'll come back. To me. Always to me.

THE END (FOR NOW)

Thank you so much for reading ***Twisted Fate***. I hope you love Damian and Alina as much as I do! Please consider leaving a review. Word of mouth is an author's best friend!

Vegas Vicious is a series of interconnected stand-alone novels about the Russo crime family.

What should you read next?

1. Double or Nothing, a Twisted Fate Bonus Epilogue (more Damian and Alina!)
2. Read the next book, Ruthless Vow (Leo and Nicole's story!)
3. Read book 3, Dark Promise

Also by Becca Kane

The Vegas Vicious Series

—Dark Mafia Romance—

Twisted Fate

Ruthless Vow

Dark Promise

Bonus Content

Double or Nothing, a Twisted Fate Bonus Epilogue

About the Author

Becca Kane is the alter ego of two acclaimed romance authors who have collectively written more than 50 novels. They have earned starred reviews, been on the New York Times bestseller list, and won numerous industry awards.

Becca writes scorching dark mafia romance about obsessive and deadly alpha heroes, their captive, gorgeous heroines, dark games, and deadly passions.

BeccaKane.com

Made in the USA
Middletown, DE
12 December 2024